You'd better watch your step, Dillon, Joe told himself. He usually had his guard up automatically when he was in the company of single women.

But with Polly? She was so open and honest, so far removed from the social set he was accustomed to. He found himself relaxing, just being himself, Joe Dillon, exactly as he was.

Oh yeah. He most definitely had better watch his step in regard to Polly Chapman. He was treading on foreign turf, where lurking in the shadows there was danger of losing his heart before he knew what hit him…

Dear Reader,

Happy Valentine's Day! What better way to celebrate this romantic day than by reading six brand-new Desires…

Jennifer Greene's *Prince Charming's Child* is February's MAN OF THE MONTH. A contemporary version of *Sleeping Beauty*, it'll certainly have you wallowing in the happy ending! In the exotic SONS OF THE DESERT title, *The Solitary Sheikh*, Alexandra Sellers brings to us a seemingly cold, hard sheikh who finds happiness with his daughters' aristocratic tutor. Eastern promise really is in the air…

A footloose cowboy renounces his wandering ways all for the sake of love in Cindy Gerard's *The Outlaw Jesse James*. And Kate Jennings finds her passionate affair with handsome marine Tom Candello's about to bear fruit… That's *Colonel Daddy*. Watch out for the next book by Maureen Child in her BACHELOR BATTALION series coming in May.

Next, the ever popular Joan Elliott Pickart brings us a wonderful love story—*Just My Joe*. Watch sparks fly between handsome, wealthy Joe Dillon and down to earth Polly. Finally, babies are on the way in Shirley Rogers's *Cowboys, Babies and Shotgun Vows*. Don't blink—you are seeing two! But how is the dad-to-be going to react to the surprising news that he's having twins?

Hoping you enjoy them all. Take care and come back next month,

The Editors

Just My Joe

JOAN ELLIOTT PICKART

SILHOUETTE
DESIRE®

First published in Great Britain 2000
Silhouette Books, Eton House, 18-24 Paradise Road,
Richmond, Surrey TW9 1SR

© Joan Elliott Pickart 1999

ISBN 0 373 76202 X

22-0002

Printed and bound in Spain
by Litografia Rosés S.A., Barcelona

JOAN ELLIOTT PICKART

is the author of over seventy novels. When she isn't writing, she enjoys watching football, knitting, reading, gardening and attending craft shows. Joan has three all-grown-up daughters and a fantastic little grandson. In September 1995, Joan travelled to China to adopt her fourth daughter, Autumn. Joan and Autumn have settled into their cozy cottage in a charming small town in the high pine country of Arizona, USA.

For Dana, a woman of courage
beyond measure.
I love you, dear friend.

One

"**C**all the cops. Call the cops."

Polly Chapman rolled her eyes heavenward as she heard the scratchy-voice command.

"Hush, Jazzy," Polly said, then pressed on the brake as she came to a red light. The ancient van she was driving shuddered and shook as it idled. "We have no need for an officer of the law." She glanced quickly around the shabby neighborhood. "Well, not at the moment, anyway. Hold that thought, though."

"Call the cops," Jazzy squawked.

"Oh, brother," Polly muttered, starting off again as the light turned green.

She shot a glare at the talkative creature in the passenger seat. Jazzy was a brightly colored and definitely opinionated macaw that was traveling in a large, bell-shaped cage. His feathers were glossy, vibrant shades of green, orange, red and yellow, and he was perched on a swing in the middle of the cage, as though determined not to miss seeing anything that might be happening.

At the next red light, Polly shifted in her seat as much as the seat belt would allow, making certain that all the doors of the vehicle were securely locked.

It had taken over an hour to drive from the northwest section of Tucson to the far south side. Now with each passing block, bleak poverty seemed to shout at her from all directions.

The buildings were old and many were decorated with sprawling graffiti, the message not always discernable. Some of the windows of stores were boarded, others whitewashed, then suddenly there would appear a store with a faded Open sign hanging on the door.

Polly frowned in dismay as she saw several people curled up in doorways, either sleeping or simply ignoring the dismal world around them. A few people strolled along the trash-cluttered sidewalk, obviously in no rush to get where they were going.

She'd heard of south Tucson, of course, but she'd never had any reason to come into this area. It had a reputation of a high crime rate, gangs on the prowl and danger. Now that she was there, she most definitely wished that she wasn't.

She glanced quickly at the map drawn on a piece of paper next to her on the seat, then began to look for street signs, many of which were missing from the metal poles.

With a sigh of relief, Polly found the street she was seeking and turned right, the map indicating that she should go five blocks to reach her destination.

A cloud settled over the sun, dropping a gray curtain on the area and emphasizing the dreary aura of the residential neighborhood she was now driving through. The houses were small, some exhibiting an attempt at pride of ownership, others seeming to shout the message of a total lack of caring.

Polly shivered, partly from the cool temperature of the overcast November day, and partly from a sense of struggle and despair that seemed to be sifting into the van and touching her with chilling fingers.

"Call the cops," Jazzy squawked.

"No, not the cops, Jazzy," Polly said quietly. "What's needed here is whole platoon of guardian angels, or fairy godmothers with magic wands."

"Silly girl," Jazzy said. "Silly girl."

"Thanks a lot," Polly said, shooting the macaw a dark glare. "I don't know why I bother to try to have a conversation with you. You're just so opinionated and judgmental."

"Fix some soup," Jazzy said.

"And sexist," Polly added. "Fix your own dumb soup. I'm not your maid." She shook her head. "Why am I talking to this bird? Just shut up, Polly Chapman."

"Polly want a cracker?" Jazzy said.

"That," she said, "is *not* funny. I could wring Robert's neck for teaching you to say that."

"Polly want a cracker?"

"No!"

Polly slowed her speed, pressed on the brake, then leaned forward for a better look, as she realized she'd found what she was searching for.

"Abraham Lincoln High School," she said aloud. "Grim, very grim."

The four-story building was obviously ancient, the red bricks crumbling at the corners and the windows having a strange yellow cast to them. There was another structure that appeared newer; it was to the right and behind the main building. The sign on the second, one-story creation announced that it was the Multipurpose Building.

"That's where we're headed, Jazzy," Polly said. "We're among the multipurpose rank and file today. Now to find somewhere to park."

It was another two blocks before Polly discovered a tight-squeeze parking place on the street. She twisted the rearview mirror to check her appearance.

That's as good as it gets, she thought. She was twenty-four years old and still got carded in bars. Nothing she tried made her look any older.

Her short, naturally curly blond hair, blue eyes and the dusting of freckles across her nose combined into a face that caused her to prove her true age time and again.

"Oh, well," she mused, with a shrug, "look at the bright side. I'll be the envy of the masses when I'm forty and look thirty. Right, Jazzy?"

"Right, Jazzy," the macaw repeated.

"Write that down. You actually agreed with something I said." Polly paused. "Well, let's trudge back to Abraham Lincoln High School. Duty calls."

"Show biz," Jazzy said. "Show biz."

"Whatever," Polly muttered.

Joe Dillon stood at one end of the Multipurpose Building, a clipboard in his hand. He was oblivious to the high volume of noise created by five hundred students talking and laughing. An army sergeant in full uniform stood in front of Joe.

"Okay," Joe said, making a check mark on the paper attached to the clipboard. "We appreciate your coming to career day, Sergeant. Just have a seat on one of those folding chairs behind the table."

The sergeant nodded and walked away.

"How are we doing, Joe?"

Joe turned to see the principal of the school. Mark Jackson was in his mid-fifties, with salt-and-pepper hair and more wrinkles on his weary face than his age indicated. He was much shorter than Joe's six feet, but Joe knew from experience that Mark was physically stronger than he appeared.

The two men not only worked together, they liked and respected each other. They were friends.

"Everyone is here except Dr. Robert Dogwood, the veterinarian. *Dog*wood? Do you suppose that's his real name?"

Mark chuckled. "Who knows? Clara and I hired a baby-sitter once whose name was Ima Nanny. She swore that was what her mother christened her. I take it you've never met Dr. Dogwood?"

Joe shook his head. "No, I just started with *A* in the yellow pages of the telephone book under Veterinarians, and hit it lucky when I got to Dogwood. People in general aren't real excited about coming into this part of town."

"True," Mark said, "and I don't blame them."

"Well, let's give the vet five more minutes to show up," Joe said. "If he doesn't make an appearance by then, we'll start without him. The troops are getting restless."

Mark swept his gaze over the crowded bleachers.

"I hope they listen," he said. "I want them to realize there's a way out of this part of town. If they'd just buckle down and study, choose a career goal, have a dream, a..." Mark sighed. "Well, this is our first attempt at a career day. There's no telling how it will be received by the students."

"Nope," Joe said, smiling. "There's no second-guessing these guys, Mark. That's just one of the things that makes teaching at Lincoln so...shall we say...challenging?"

Mark laughed. "That's a polite word for it. But you and I sign new contracts every year. We're either dedicated, or dumb." His smile faded. "Who am I kidding? We belong here, honestly believe we might make a difference, reach a few of these frustrated, angry kids."

"Yep," Joe said, nodding. "I'm not going anywhere. I'm in for the long haul."

"And I'm grateful for that," Mark said. "I'd hate to be doing this without you on my staff."

"Don't get mushy on me, Mark." Joe glanced toward the door at the other end of the building. "Well, Dr. Dogwood is a no-show, I guess. So, let the games begin."

"All right. I'll quiet the inmates down, then turn the microphone over to you, since you're the one who coordinated the whole thing."

"Go for it," Joe said, then watched the principal walk away.

Mark was a good man, he thought. He'd grown up in a neighborhood like this one in Detroit, understood these students and what they were up against. He and his family lived in a nice home on the northwest side, but Mark was dedicated to helping these kids, would stay at Lincoln until he retired.

Joe swept his gaze over the noisy crowd.

And Joe Dillon? he mused. He came from a far different upbringing. His family was wealthy and he'd had every materialistic whim met and then some. He'd taken it all for granted. He wanted it, he got it, no questions asked, and the image of it all in his mind made him cringe.

Ten years ago he'd decided it was payback time. He'd walked away from the world of money, except for the occasional appearances at megabucks events to keep his parents happy.

He worked in the ghetto. Lived in the ghetto. Breathed the air in the ghetto. It was the only way to really relate to these kids, be the kind of teacher he was determined to be. He lacked Mark's firsthand knowledge of this life, but he was making up for it in his own way.

Sacrifices? Joe mentally wandered on. Yeah, sure, he'd made sacrifices. The biggest one, he supposed, was the fact that he would never marry and have a family. He couldn't ask a wife and children to live down here and he had every intention of staying. So be it.

As the years went by, he had less patience and tolerance for the idle rich, the jet-set crowd, those who refused to address anything beyond their selfish pleasures. They pretended that neighborhoods like this one, kids like these, didn't exist. Damn.

Enough, Dillon, he told himself. The vet had obviously gotten cold feet. It was time to get this show on the road.

The two-block walk back to the school seemed more like twenty to Polly as the weight of Jazzy's heavy cage began to make her hand, arm and shoulder ache.

Arriving at last outside the wide double doors of the Multipurpose Building, Polly stopped to catch her breath and regain her composure. She blew a puff of air up over her face, ruffling the curls on her forehead.

"Well, here we go, Jazzy," she said.

She pulled open one of the doors and stepped inside

to hear an amplified man's voice say, "...who put in many hours to make this career day at Abraham Lincoln possible. Ladies and gentlemen, please show your appreciation to our own Coach Dillon."

Polly took another step, then stopped dead in her tracks with a gasp of shock as the student's *appreciation* erupted at full volume. They applauded, hooted and hollered, stamped their feet in a rumbling rhythm on the bleachers and whistled shrilly.

"Good grief," Polly muttered, then frowned.

Heavens, she thought, she had to cover the entire length of the building to reach the ever-famous and much-appreciated Coach Dillon and the other people, who were seated on folding chairs. With a chatty bird in a cage, she was about to parade in front of several hundred students.

"Thank you," Joe said, raising both hands for silence.

Polly started tentatively forward.

The students quieted slowly, then silence fell.

Polly lifted her chin and kept moving.

"The purpose of this first career day at Lincoln," Joe continued, "is to give all of you the opportunity to..."

"Call the cops," Jazzy squawked, loud and clear.

The students whooped with laughter.

"No way, Bird Lady," a boy shouted. "The cops come calling on me more than I want to see them."

Polly felt a warm flush stain her cheeks as she quickened her step, mentally clicking off ways to murder Jazzy.

What in the hell... Joe thought frowning, as the noise level increased to full volume again. Who was this? It sure wasn't the Dr. Robert Dogwood he'd spoken to on the telephone. It was some kid with a talking bird, who had managed to totally disrupt the program before it had hardly begun.

No, wait a minute. The girl had to have been sent by the vet. Otherwise, it didn't make any sense for her to be here. He didn't envy her the walk she was making, that was for sure. Well, she was getting closer now and…

Whoa, Joe thought. That wasn't a kid, it was most definitely a woman. A very pretty—in a fresh, wholesome way—woman. She was wearing pale blue slacks that defined her feminine curves and a dark blue blouse that hinted at womanly breasts beneath it.

Oh, yes, she was young, but she was a woman, no doubt about it. He was going to take pity on her and escort her past the remaining students.

Joe came from behind the table and strode toward the woman carrying the birdcage, his long legs covering the distance in short order.

Polly stopped and looked up at the man she now knew to be Coach Dillon.

"I…" she began, then forgot what she was about to say.

My stars, she thought. In the midst of this embarrassing chaos she was in close proximity to one of the most ruggedly handsome men she'd ever seen.

Oh, yes, one certainly should *appreciate* Coach Dillon. He was tall, with wide shoulders, his chiseled features were tan, his dark brown hair thick and in need of a trim, and his yummy eyes were the color of fudge sauce.

"I'm sorry I'm late," Polly said, amazed she had enough air in her lungs to speak. "I couldn't find a place to park and I had to walk a couple of blocks. This cage is heavy, so I had to set it down once and…"

"You're not Dr. Dogwood," Joe said, frowning. Very, *very* pretty, now that he was close enough for a full perusal. But how old was she? Twenty? Twenty-two? Twenty-five? He really couldn't tell. "I'm assuming he sent you, though?"

"Yes. Robert had an emergency surgery to perform. His wife, Dr. Nancy Dogwood, is covering the appointments at the clinic. I'm Ms. Polly Chapman, a veterinary technician."

"I see," Joe said.

"I've never done anything like this before. I have no idea what you want me to say, Coach Dillon. Robert didn't have time to explain things to me."

"It's Joe…Polly. You won't be first on the program, so you'll have a chance to hear some of the others speak before it's your turn. May I carry your bird for you?"

"What? Oh. Yes, thank you."

Polly lifted Jazzy's cage and Joe slid his fingers through the brass ring at the top, brushing Polly's fingers as she released her hold. A sudden and startling heat exploded from the feathery touch, shooting up both Polly and Joe's arms.

Their eyes collided with matching confusion; summer-sky blue eyes and eyes of fudge-sauce brown.

"Wanna snuggle, bunny?" Jazzy squawked.

Polly snapped her head around to glare at the bird.

"Jazzy, for heaven's sake," she scolded, "hush."

Joe spun on his heel and strode back to the area containing the table and chairs, Polly following more slowly behind him.

Gracious, she thought, what a strange sensation that had been when her hand had met with Joe Dillon's. She could *still* feel the heat tingling along her arm and across her breasts.

It was probably static electricity.

No, she thought, in the next instant. That was an easy-out explanation, but she somehow knew it wasn't true. It had been a man-woman thing, a sensuous something, that was disconcerting, to say the least.

Joe Dillon was one of those dangerous men who oozed blatant masculinity by doing nothing more than standing there. He was the type who had to beat women off with a stick. Oh, yes, Joe was very, *very* dangerous.

Polly settled onto a folding chair, smiled politely at the people on either side of her, then nodded her thanks to Joe as he set Jazzy's cage on the floor in front of her. She folded her hands primly in her lap and plastered what she hoped was a pleasant, professional expression on her face.

Only then did she realize she was seated directly behind Joe, where he was now standing at the microphone on the table.

My, my, Polly thought, such delectable scenery. Coach Dillon certainly did have a nice tush, and those long, beautifully muscled legs weren't too shabby, either. The man just didn't quit. He had it all, from head to toe.

Oh, goodness, there was that heat again, only this time it was traveling in the opposite direction, swirling low within her. This would never do. She didn't have reactions like this to men she'd known for about three seconds. She didn't have reactions like this to men she'd known for three *years*.

Enough was enough. She was going to quit staring at Joe Dillon's buns and get herself back under control.

Slowly and admittedly a tad reluctantly, Polly shifted her gaze to the side wall of the building, where a huge, snarling head of a bear had been painted with vivid yellow and blue colors. Beneath the bear was the block-letter word *Grizzlies*.

That must be the school mascot, Polly thought absently. The Abraham Lincoln Grizzlies. How nice. The years in high school were such fun. But then again, maybe they weren't for the kids in this neighborhood. That was a depressing thought.

"Polly want a cracker?" Jazzy said.

"Shh," she whispered, nudging the cage with her toe.

Joe fiddled with the papers he'd picked up from the table, then cleared his throat.

Lord, he thought, he felt like he'd been punched in the gut. When his fingers had slid over Polly Chapman's, heat had rocketed up his arm, then slammed into his lower body.

That wholesome-looking, freckles-on-her-cute-nose woman had had a potent impact on him. He wasn't accustomed to things like that happening to him, and he didn't like it, not one damn bit.

Cripes, Polly wasn't even his type. He didn't keep company with women who looked like they could be a model for a box of cornflakes. He dated savvy gals, the single scene game players who knew the rules. No one got hurt, and a good time was had by all.

Enough mental talking to yourself, Dillon, he thought. If he didn't get this show on the road, he'd have a mutiny on his hands. The natives of Lincoln High were definitely getting restless.

"Okay, ladies and gentlemen," he said, speaking into the microphone, "settle down, please."

"Bring on the Bird Lady, Coach," a boy yelled. "We want the Bird Lady."

The students cheered and stamped their feet, obviously in favor of the hollered request.

Oh, dear heaven, Polly thought, the building was going to fall down. All those stamping feet pounding on the bleachers was creating a deafening roar. Well, Joe Dillon, who must coach something or other, better not make her speak before the others, because she had absolutely no idea what to say.

"Chill," Joe said, slicing one hand through the air. "Now."

Silence fell so quickly it was as though someone had pulled the plug on a boom box.

"All right," Joe said. "This career day is being presented for you, and I respect the fact that you should have some say in how it's conducted. Therefore, please welcome Ms. Polly Chapman."

Joe turned and smiled at Polly, who glowered at him and stayed glued to her chair. Joe closed the short distance between them and bent over slightly to speak to her.

"Look, I'm sorry," he said. "If I try to cram this program down their throats they'll tune out from word one. You've peaked their curiosity and that's terrific."

"Terrific?" Polly said, raising her eyebrows. "What am I supposed to say?"

"Just tell them what you do and the kind of training it required to be able to do whatever it is you do." Joe shrugged. "Wing it." He chuckled. "That wasn't a pun, Bird Lady."

"Cute," Polly muttered.

Joe smiled his best hundred-watt smile, picked up Jazzy's cage and returned to the table, placing the cage in front of the microphone.

"Oh, dear, dear," Polly mumbled, getting to her feet.

Joe stepped back to allow Polly access to the microphone. Polly moved to the table, then out of the corner of her eye she saw Joe settle onto the chair she'd vacated.

Her eyes widened as she remembered the clear view of Joe's tush she'd had while sitting in that chair. She was going to have enough difficulty talking to this rowdy audience without knowing that Joe Dillon was probably indulging in a thorough scrutiny of her bottom.

Polly spun around. "You can't sit there."

"Why not?" Joe asked, confusion evident on his face.

"Because you're making me nervous by sitting there."

"Why? A chair, is a chair, is a chair."

"Shoo," Polly said, flapping her hands at him. "Go somewhere else."

Joe planted his hands on his thighs and pushed himself to his feet.

"Yes, ma'am," he said. "Whatever you say, ma'am."

"Thank you," Polly said, then turned back to the microphone.

Joe sat down again in his chair.

"Good morning," Polly said, sweeping her gaze over the students. "I'm Polly Chapman and I'd like to thank you for inviting me here."

Ho-ho, Joe thought. No wonder Polly was all in a flutter about his having taken up residency in her chair. The pretty lady had executed a perusal of his butt, and figured he'd do the same to her.

How right she was.

And what a nice, feminine bottom Ms. Chapman had.

An instant later Joe frowned as he felt that heat again, that damnable heat, coiling deep and low within him.

This was ridiculous, he thought, with self-disgust. His

body was reacting to Polly Chapman the way one of his students with a hormone rush might.

He wasn't a randy seventeen-year-old, for Pete's sake. He was a mature, in control, thirty-three-year-old man. The absurd effect Polly was having on him was becoming very, *very* tiresome.

So, quit staring at the woman's delectable rear end, Joe ordered himself.

He shifted his gaze to the back of Polly's head and immediately wondered what those silky-appearing, blond curls would feel like sliding through his fingers.

That's it, he thought, getting to his feet. He'd definitely had enough of sitting in this chair.

Joe moved to the end of the table and crossed his arms over his chest. Polly looked at him questioningly.

"Carry on," he said. "Ignore me."

Oh, right, she thought dryly. About the last thing a woman would be able to do in regard to Mr. Masculinity Personified Dillon was to ignore him. He was so male and so incredibly *there*.

"Yes, well," Polly said, directing her attention to the students again, "ever since I was a little girl I wanted to be a veterinarian. I was always toting home dogs, cats, birds, frogs, anything and everything that I was convinced needed my tender loving care.

"That dream for my future career didn't dim as I grew older, but I had to face reality. The amount of money it would take to become a vet was far beyond my reach. Even with the numerous resources available for student loans, my dream was not obtainable."

Joe swept his gaze over the students, seeing their rapt attention, hearing the total silence as five hundred pairs of eyes remained riveted on Polly.

She had them, he thought. These kids knew, they un-

derstood, about dreams that would never come true.
*Keep talking, Polly. They're listening to every word
you're saying.*

"To my utmost joy," Polly continued, "I discovered
a program of study at the University of Arizona that
would enable me to become a veterinary technician in
half the time and less than half the cost of the veterinary
medicine program.

"So, I looked at the bright side, saw a way to be
included in the career arena I'd dreamed about, even if
it wasn't in the capacity I had initially hoped for. For
several years now I've been employed by Dr. Robert and
Dr. Nancy Dogwood, a husband-and-wife veterinarian
team who have an office on the northwest side of town."

"So what do they let you do, Bird Lady?" someone
yelled. "Poop scoop after the dogs and cats have been
there?"

Polly laughed. "Sometimes. But I'm capable of giving examinations, inoculations, doing follow-up treat-
ment of animals who have had surgery—and the list
goes on. It's very rewarding, very fulfilling."

"That's cool," a girl said. "So, what's with the
bird?"

"This is Jazzy," Polly said. "In addition to their regular practice, the Dogwoods also offer a boarding service
for pets. I thought it might be fun to bring Jazzy with
me today. His owners are in Europe for six months."

"Oh, ain't that a shame?" a boy quipped.

Be careful, Polly, Joe mentally directed. *Don't cross
over the line into a world where these kids will never
go. Don't lose them now.*

Polly flipped open the door of the cage and Jazzy
hopped out onto the table.

"Jazzy is a macaw," Polly said. "Some of you heard

him speak earlier. He has an uncanny knack of saying things that fit the moment, making a person believe, at times, that he's carrying on a conversation. That, of course, is impossible. Anyway, I took extra classes in the care of exotic birds after the Dogwoods hired me, because they board an amazing number of them during the year.''

"Give me a kiss, hot stuff," Jazzy squawked.

"How much does one of those fancy birds cost?" a girl asked.

Uh-oh, Joe thought.

"Jazzy comes from a long line of champion macaws," Polly said pleasantly. "He's worth..."

Don't say it, Polly, Joe silently begged. *Tell them you have no idea what the stupid bird is valued at.*

"...I'd say," Polly said, "probably several thousands of dollars."

Oh, hell, Joe thought.

Polly blinked in surprise as the students erupted in boos, whistles and thumbs-down gestures.

What was going on? she thought frantically. The students had been listening to her; she knew they had. They'd been sincerely interested in what she had been saying. What had suddenly gone wrong?

Joe stepped in front of the table and raised his hands.

"Quiet down," he shouted. "Knock it off. I understand where you're coming from, but there's no excuse for being rude."

Well, she was glad Joe understood where the now angry and obviously upset students were "coming from," Polly thought, wrapping her hands around her elbows in a protective gesture. She didn't have a clue.

"You're pushing me," Joe hollered. "Knock...it... off."

Then Polly watched in wide-eyed horror as Jazzy waddled to the edge of the front of the table, ruffled his feathers, then proceeded to bite Joe Dillon on the right side of his oh-so-gorgeous tush!

Two

It was bedlam.

Joe roared as the message of a sudden, sharp pain reached his brain, then he spun around, fury very evident on his face. Jazzy made a beeline for the cage and hustled inside. Polly quickly shut and locked the door.

The students went wild; laughing, hooting, pointing at Joe in obvious delight at what had transpired. The pounding of feet on the bleachers began again and three cheers of hip, hip, hooray were executed in Jazzy's honor.

I want to go home, Polly thought frantically.

Mark Jackson left his chair and came to the table.

"I'll take over," he told Joe. "You'd better exit stage left with Ms. Chapman and the felon." He grinned. "Do you need to see a doctor about your wound?"

"No," Joe said, his jaw tight. "I need to find a recipe for barbecued macaw."

"That's not fair," Polly said. "Jazzy was upset by the noise and acted out of character. He has never bitten anyone before. He was shook-up and your...your posterior was right in front of him and..."

"Save it," Joe said gruffly.

He snatched up the cage, then came around the table to grip Polly's upper arm.

"We're outta here," he said.

"Bye, Bird Lady," a chorus of students sang out. "Bye, Jazzy."

Polly smiled and waggled the fingers of her free hand in farewell. In the next instant she was nearly lifted off her feet as Joe began to haul her toward the side entrance to the building. Mark Jackson stepped up to the microphone.

"Okay, we've had some fun," the principal said, "but it's time to get serious. Quiet down. Our next speaker is..."

Before Polly knew the identity of the next speaker, she was propelled outside, the door clanging shut behind her, Jazzy and Joe. Joe set the cage on the ground, then rubbed the area of his anatomy that had been attacked.

"Damn it, that really hurt," he said, glowering at Polly. "Not only that, but your stupid bird made me look like a fool in front of the students."

"It wasn't Jazzy's fault." Polly poked her nose in the air and folded her arms beneath her breasts. "He was frightened. I mean, heavens, so was I. One minute I was giving my nifty little speech and the next thing I knew the students went berserk. What did I do wrong?"

Joe sighed and picked up the cage.

"Come on, Polly," he said. "I'll walk you to your car. I purposely invited men to be the speakers today. I know there's limited parking around the school, and it wasn't my intention to have a woman wandering alone in this section of town.''

Polly laughed. "No one would dare bother me. I have an attack bird for protection.'' She glanced up at Joe's stormy expression. "Sorry. I was just trying to lighten the mood here. Look at the bright side, Joe. Jazzy could have clamped on to your...your person and refused to let go. Now *that* would have been very embarrassing.'' She nodded decisively.

"Your car, Polly?" Joe said, no hint of a smile on his face.

Polly moved around him. "Okay, fine. It's two blocks away.''

Joe fell in step beside Polly as they left the school grounds. Jazzy was blessedly silent.

"Well?" Polly asked finally, after they'd gone a half a block without speaking. "Are you going to tell me what giant mistake I made during my speech?''

"You don't have even the slightest clue, do you?" Joe glared at Polly, then shook his head. "You just don't get it.''

"Obviously not.''

"Look, you started out just fine, really great, in fact. You hit those kids where they live with your story of having a dream, but realizing you didn't have the financial resources to achieve it. You definitely had their interest and full attention.''

"Hooray for me,'' Polly said dryly. "It sure didn't last long.''

"You were stopped short of your goal, your dream,'' Joe continued, "but found a way to be connected to the field you wanted to be in. Then? Hell, you blew it.''

"What did I do?" Polly said, nearly yelling.

"Jazzy's owners are in Europe for six months? This

stupid bird cost thousands of dollars? Come on, Polly, get real."

"What I said was true."

"And that's the problem. Don't you see?" Joe said, none too quietly. "In the eyes of those kids you sold out. You struggled, you settled for less than you originally dreamed of, then you ran, did not walk, into the world of the idle rich."

"That's ridiculous," Polly said. "The Dogwoods offered me a job and I took it. That's what most people do when they need to pay the rent and buy food. What difference does it make where I'm employed to enable me to use the skills I worked so hard to obtain?"

"It makes a very big difference, Ms. Chapman. You could be with an open veterinary clinic in a low-income neighborhood. Or the Humane Society. Or be the veterinary technician for one of those organizations that finds families for homeless animals.

"But, oh, no, not you. You're baby-sitting idiot birds that cost more than some of those kids' parents make in six months. You copped out on your roots, on who you are, and those students knew it."

"Call the cops," Jazzy said. "Call the cops."

Polly stopped walking, causing Joe to halt his step. She looked up at him, her blue eyes flashing with anger.

"Wait just a minute here," she said. "You agree with those kids, don't you? You're expressing your own views about me, as well as theirs. Right? Isn't that right, Joe? You're standing in judgment of me, just like those students did."

"Damn straight I am. You were in a position to give something back to the world you came from. Instead? You're hobnobbing with the rich and famous, who go to Europe for six months and think spending thousands of dollars on a bird is chump change. Yeah, I agree with the students of Abraham Lincoln High School. You sold out, Polly Chapman.''

''And you're certifiably insane, Joe Dillon.''

Polly spun around and started off again. Joe strode after her.

''Totally nuts, that's what you are,'' Polly raged on. ''Oh-h-h, you're infuriating. How dare you pass judgment on me? You've got a lot of nerve, do you know that? I work very hard for my paycheck and… No, forget it. I'm not justifying myself and my existence to you. You don't know the first thing about me.''

''I know every word you said in your crummy speech, lady.''

''Well, excuse me to hell and back for making a living, Mr. Dillon, for keeping a roof over my head and food on my table.''

''Hell, I can't get through to you, make you understand. I'm wasting my breath.''

''Oh, yes, do save your breath. I'm sure it takes an extra dose to be so full of hot air.'' Polly executed an indignant little sniff. ''You talk the talk, but do you walk the walk?''

''Meaning?''

''Does the lack of a wedding ring on your hand indicate that you're single?''

''Yes.''

''So, you're a single man, who has probably been teaching for a dozen years, or more. I imagine that adds up to what would be considered a sizable salary in this particular neighborhood.

''You arrive at Abraham Lincoln high every morning with your holier-than-thou attitude. But at day's end?

What part of town do you drive home to, Joe? What cushy, comfortable section of Tucson do you live in?"

Polly stomped off the curb and around to the driver's side of her van, pulling her keys from her pocket as she went.

"Well, that question is easy enough to answer," Joe said, coming up behind her.

Polly unlocked the door. "Do tell."

"What a convenient coincidence. You're parked in front of the house I rent. *This* is the cushy part of Tucson where I reside, Ms. Chapman. I talk the talk and, by damn, I walk the walk."

Polly opened her mouth with every intention of telling Joe that his sense of humor left a lot to be desired. She snapped her mouth closed again in the next instant, as the thought struck her that maybe he wasn't kidding about her being parked in front of his house.

She moved to the left to enable her to see the structure in question clearly, her eyes widening.

The house was a small wood frame with several different-colored shingles on the roof. It was obviously old, but appeared well cared for. It was painted beige with dark brown trim, had a narrow porch that held two lawn chairs, and the minuscule front yard was covered in dark brown-colored gravel.

It was, without a doubt, Polly decided, the most tended-to looking house on the block, but that still didn't mean it was where Joe Dillon lived. It just didn't make one iota of sense for a man with his income to live in this high-crime part of town.

"You don't believe me, do you?" Joe said.

"I'm thinking it over," Polly said, still staring at the house. "I simply can't get a grip on why you would choose to live…well, in the ghetto if you don't have to.''

She looked at Joe, a puzzled expression on her face.

"The career day you organized at the school,'' she continued, ''is proof that you want your students to have hopes and dreams of a better life. You were attempting to show them that there *are* ways to get out of this environment. Why, Joe? Why would you intentionally remain here if you aren't forced to?''

Polly shifted her gaze back to the house. ''No, I'm not certain I believe that you live here. There's no rhyme or reason for it.''

"Come on,'' Joe said. ''I'll prove it to you.''

"Don't you have classes to teach?''

"The career day assembly will last all morning. I'll be back at the school in time for my next scheduled class. Are you coming?''

"Why not?'' Polly said, throwing up her hands. ''So far my day has been totally bizarre. What's one more layer on the cake?''

"Cake and ice cream,'' Jazzy said, ''and a bottle of beer.''

"That's a gross combination, Jazzy,'' Polly said.

"Polly want a cracker?'' the bird said.

"Oh, hush,'' she said.

"I suppose I'd better hold on to this cage and not put it in the van,'' Joe said. ''After all, this mound of feathers is worth thousands of dollars.''

"Don't start that again,'' Polly said, frowning. ''*I'm* not the one who determined the monetary worth of champion-line macaws.''

"No, you're just the one who baby-sits them while the owners are in Europe for six months.'' Joe moved past her and started toward the house. "What a terrific contribution to society you make, Ms. Chapman."

Polly sighed and followed Joe up the cracked, cement sidewalk leading to the little house.

On the porch, Joe raised one eyebrow and cocked his head toward the black metal mailbox mounted next to the door. The name *Dillon* was spelled out on the front of the mailbox in white, stick-on letters. He removed some keys from his pocket.

"All right," Polly said. "That's enough. I believe that you live here. I can't fathom why you do, but I'll concede that this is your house."

"Don't you want a tour of the mansion?"

"I'm not in the habit of entering the homes of strange men I don't even know," she said, with a little sniff. "And you, sir, are very strange."

Joe chuckled despite his determination not to. A funny shiver fluttered down Polly's spine at the sound of the deep, masculine rumble. The smile that had touched Joe's lips disappeared in the next second.

"Like I said, you just don't get it," he said. "How can I relate to my students, really understand them, if I don't live in the reality of their world?"

He narrowed his eyes as he looked directly at Polly.

"You?" he said. "You function in a sphere of wealth, cater to the rich, who indulge themselves in such nonsense as expensive birds for pets.

"You rose above what were obviously humble beginnings, then *turned* your back on your reality, instead of *giving* something back. Am I even close to getting through to you, Polly?"

"You're coming across loud and clear," she said. "You're a judgmental, narrow-minded man, with a mind-set that isn't open for any kind of discussion. You pass censure on people you don't even know, having no clue as to their personal circumstances.''

"I..."

"Guess what, Joe Dillon? I don't like you. You might be the most blatantly sexy man I've ever met, but big macho deal. Give me the bird, Joe.''

"What?" Joe said, with a burst of laughter.

"You know what I mean," Polly said, snatching the heavy cage from Joe's hand. "I'm leaving. Now. I suppose I should be polite and say it was a pleasure to meet you, but it wasn't. This entire experience has been grim. Goodbye, Mr. Dillon.''

Joe frowned as Polly left the porch and started down the sidewalk, heading for the van.

"Polly, wait," he said.

"No!"

Joe watched as Polly maneuvered the van carefully out of the tight parking space. He had a smile and a wave ready to execute if Polly should glance back in his direction.

But she didn't.

And within minutes she had chugged out of his view in the rattling vehicle.

With a sigh and a shake of his head, Joe sank onto one of the lawn chairs and dragged both hands down his face.

Lord, he was jerk, he thought, in self-disgust. Yes, he believed in what he was doing by living in the ghetto so as to better understand the students he taught who existed in this environment. He'd called this little frame house his home for nearly ten years.

But he'd hammered his convictions at Polly, had jumped all over her like a fanatic who gave no quarter to anyone's opinion that didn't match his own.

He'd been a totally obnoxious, overbearing, narrow-minded jerk.

Joe rested his elbows on his knees, laced his fingers loosely together and stared into space.

He knew why he'd behaved the way he had toward Polly Chapman. She'd picked up the price tag for the previous evening spent at his parents' house. The hours with his folks had been worse than usual, and he'd arrived home wired, angry, unable to sleep for more than snatches at a time during the long night.

So what did he do? He slam-dunked the first person who crossed his path who even hinted at embracing the world of money. Damn.

Polly had not deserved the way he had treated her. So, okay, he believed she *had* sold out, was catering to the idle rich when she was in a position to give something back to the world she had come from.

But Polly had been right when she'd accused him of passing judgment on her without knowing her personal circumstances. He'd never done that to anyone before and he definitely felt like the scum of the earth for doing it to Polly.

With a muttered expletive, Joe planted his hands on his thighs and pushed himself to his feet.

He had to apologize to Polly, he thought, stepping off the porch. He still believed in what he'd said, but that didn't excuse the way he'd said it. It was a conditional apology, he supposed, but one that definitely needed to be extended.

"What a lousy day," he said aloud, as he began his trek back to the school. "Polly want a cracker? No, Polly Chapman would probably like to punch me right in the nose."

* * *

Polly was so furious that she was halfway back to the office before she realized it. She blinked, telling herself to pay attention to the surging traffic, then sighed as a wave of fatigue swept over her.

She wasn't accustomed to engaging in confrontations like the one she'd had with Joe Dillon. It had left her emotionally drained, so exhausted she could weep.

She had to forget it, push the disturbing memories from her mind, along with the lingering images of Joe. The entire morning and the people involved in it were going to be erased from her brain.

Somehow.

"Give me the bird, Joe," Jazzy squawked. "Joe. Joe. Give me the bird."

"Oh, great, just dandy," Polly said, shooting a glare at the macaw. "Shut up, Jazzy."

"Shut up, Jazzy. Give me the bird, Joe."

Polly mumbled a very unladylike word and forced herself to concentrate on her driving.

Doctors Nancy and Robert Dogwood were an attractive, friendly couple in their early forties. They'd chosen not to have children, stating that their maternal and paternal instincts were lavished on the animals they cared for. They were both standing by the receptionist's desk when Polly entered the office.

"There they are," Robert said, smiling. "Our ambassadors to Abraham Lincoln High School. How did it go, Polly?"

Polly hoisted the heavy cage up onto the counter.

"Give me the bird, Joe," Jazzy squawked.

"I beg your pardon?" Nancy said, laughing. "That's a new one. I hope he forgets it before his owners return. So, Polly? Who's Joe?"

"It must be Joe Dillon," Robert said, "the teacher who called to ask if I'd speak at the career day assembly. You don't look too happy, Polly. Did something go wrong at the school?"

"Everything went wrong," Polly said miserably. She plunked her elbows on the counter and rested her chin in her hands. "Students in that part of town get a tad hostile when you tell them a bird costs thousands of dollars and its owners are gallivanting around Europe."

"Whew," Robert said. "I never thought of that. I'm sure I would have rattled off the same information if I had given the speech."

"Yes, well, Joe Dillon seemed to think I should have known better than to divulge that data. He was *not* pleased with me. Then to add spice to the soup, Jazzy bit Joe on the tush in front of all the students."

"Oh, good heavens," Nancy said, laughing. "You poor dear. What an awful morning you've had."

Polly nodded, mentally cataloging the things she couldn't, wouldn't, share with her employers, who were also her friends.

To relate how Joe Dillon had accused her of selling out by working for the Dogwoods was a direct, negative reflection on the doctors themselves. *That* they definitely didn't need to hear.

And she certainly wasn't confessing to the strange, sensual reaction she'd had to Joe Dillon, nor the fact that there was *still* a lingering heat simmering within her that had been caused by Joe's touch.

"Go to lunch, Polly," Robert said. "You look done in. I sincerely apologize for sending you to the school in my place."

"It wasn't your fault it was a disaster." Polly glanced at the empty chair that belonged to the receptionist.

"Don't you want me to cover the phone, per usual, while Becky is at lunch?"

"I'll do it," Nancy said. "We're on schedule here. The next appointment isn't for an hour. We're waiting for the restaurant to deliver Pookie's food."

"Pookie the poodle is having her meals catered by a restaurant while she's boarding here?" Polly said.

"Yep," Robert said, smiling. "Isn't that a hoot? No ordinary canned dog food for that pooch. Today she's having custom-made dog food and a few thin slices of medium-rare steak. Do you think she'd notice if I ate the steak?"

"She'd notice," Nancy said. "Don't you dare take one bite of that meat when it arrives."

Catered restaurant meals for a poodle? Polly thought incredulously. How many of Joe Dillon's students had ever had thinly sliced steak, or eaten in a place fancy enough to serve it? *She'd* never even dined in an establishment like that.

If the students at Abraham Lincoln High School knew about Pookie's culinary delights, Joe would probably have a riot on his hands.

"Don't...don't you think that this nonsense about Pookie's food is a bit much?" she asked.

Robert shrugged. "The Hendersons can afford it. Pookie is like a child to them. They never would have boarded her if it wasn't for a family emergency back east. They've already called twice to check on their little darling. Once from the airport and then from the plane, thirty thousand feet up in the clouds."

"Oh, good grief," Polly said.

"I think it's sweet," Nancy said. "We see our share of abused and abandoned animals. The Hendersons love

Pookie and have no qualms about letting it be known how they feel about her. There's no harm in that.''

"But…'' Polly began, then stopped speaking and pressed her fingertips to her throbbing temples. "Forget it. I have a killer headache, my mind is mush, and the events of this morning are a nightmare I intend to erase from my memory bank.''

"Go to lunch and take extra time," Nancy said.

"Yes, all right," Polly said. "I'll get my brown bag from the refrigerator and go eat in the park. That ought to fix me right up.''

"Give me the bird, Joe," Jazzy hollered.

"Oops," Robert said, lifting Jazzy's cage from the counter. "You're going out of sight, Jazzy. Polly definitely has murder on her agenda in regard to you. Come on, I'll give you a piece of apple.''

"Apple," Jazzy repeated. "Apple and a bottle of beer.''

Robert left the reception area with the chattering bird.

"Polly, are you really all right?" Nancy asked, frowning. "You're awfully pale.''

"I'll be fine," she said, managing to produce a small smile. "This morning's adventure was rather unsettling, that's all. After some food and bit of peace and quiet in the park, I'll be as good as new.''

The bell over the door chimed as someone entered the office.

"Oh, here's Pookie's lunch," Nancy said.

"I'm gone." Polly hurried away in the direction of the back room where her packed lunch was waiting in the refrigerator. "Thinly sliced steak? Cripes, I'm having peanut butter and jelly.''

Three

The next morning, Polly sat at the round wooden table placed in front of the windows at one end of her narrow kitchen.

Sipping from a mug of hot tea, she willed the brew to infuse her with energy, render her wide-awake and ready to face the new day with vigor and enthusiasm.

It didn't work.

She plunked her elbows on the table, nestled her chin in her hands, then closed her eyes.

She was so-o-o tired, she thought. She'd hardly slept last night, had tossed and turned for hours. When she *did* manage to doze off she'd dreamed about Joe Dillon, the rotten bum.

In one of her dumb dreams, Joe had been decked out in a tuxedo and was waltzing with a six-foot macaw wearing a top hat. The bird was the same colors as Jazzy and she knew, just knew, that the trouble-making crea-

ture had been in subconscious cahoots with Joe to rob
her of blissful, peaceful slumber.

But then the scene had shifted to a misty clearing in
a wood. The trees had leaves of glittering silver that
shimmered like a million stars.

Joe was still wearing the tuxedo, but this time *she* was
his dance partner, emerging from the ring of magical
trees in a gorgeous, full-length dress to step into his em-
brace.

Polly sighed wistfully as she allowed the dream to
replay in her mind like a movie.

What an elegant couple they made as they waltzed to
music that was floating over them from a source un-
known.

Even now, in the light of the new day, she could remember the heat of passion that had suffused her in the
dream, and could vividly recall the desire radiating from
Joe's compelling brown eyes as he kept his gaze riveted
on her.

He'd dipped his head and she'd known, and gloried
in the fact, that he was about to claim her lips in what
would be a searing kiss.

Closer and closer his lips had come to hers. Closer
and closer and then…

"I woke up," Polly said, opening her eyes and smack-
ing the table with the palm of one hand. "Drat. No,
forget it. I wouldn't want to kiss that grouchy, opinionated man anyway."

Joe Dillon was a menace. He was totally disrupting
her peace of mind. Granted, her quiet lunch in the park
yesterday had soothed her jangled nerves regarding the
angry outburst from the students at Lincoln high.

She understood why she'd upset those kids, although
she still felt it wasn't her fault. She should have been
coached about what to say, or not say, before being

thrown unprepared on the mercy of the Abraham Lincoln Grizzlies.

So, live and learn, and put the disastrous morning behind her. Fine. But as she'd left the pretty park to return to the office, the image of Joe came with her and refused to budge from her mental vision for the remainder of the day.

And the long, long hours of the night.

"Darn him," Polly said.

She sipped some more tea, then swept her gaze over her small apartment. From where she was sitting she could see the living room, with its sofa, easy chair, rocker and television set. Out of her view was the bedroom and bathroom.

The sofa and chair were a splash of vibrantly colored flowers. The rocker was the one her mother had used to lull her babies to sleep.

This was usually one of her favorite times of the day in her little abode, she thought, with the morning sun streaming in the sparkling clean windows, touching everything with a warm, golden glow.

But not today.

Not with Joe Dillon still haunting her, seeming so close, so real, she might as well offer him a cup of tea.

Why? she thought, aware of a bubble of anger growing within her.

Why couldn't she dismiss Joe Dillon, along with the memories of the fiasco at the school?

Why could she still feel that incredible heat that had suffused her when their hands had brushed against each other?

Why could she hear that rumbly, sexy chuckle of Joe's, see those fathomless fudge-sauce-colored eyes, his wide shoulders, muscled legs and that—shame on her— gorgeous, tight tush?

Why was Joe Dillon having such a lingering, disturbing, sensual, *ridiculous* impact on her?

"Darned if I know," Polly said aloud, then drained her mug. "But I've had enough of this nonsense. Have you got that, Dillon? Get out of my brain space."

Dandy, she thought dryly, getting to her feet. Now she was talking to the man as though he were actually there in her kitchen. She was off to work to spend the day with lovely animals who wouldn't do, or say, anything that would further boggle her mind.

And she wasn't going anywhere near gabby Jazzy.

The morning at the office was busy, the appointment book fully scheduled.

Just before noon, a frantic man came rushing in the door with his yowling cat wrapped in a fluffy pink towel. The feline proceeded to calmly deliver three kittens on one of the examining tables. Polly had to wave an ammonia stick beneath the man's nose to keep him from passing out cold on his face.

Becky went to lunch and Polly settled onto the receptionist's chair to answer the telephone for the next hour.

Nancy and Robert came up behind Polly to take a look at the appointment book that would tell them what was on the agenda for the afternoon.

The bell over the door chimed as someone entered the office.

"Oh, Robert," Nancy said, "are those for me? What's the occasion? Did I forget something important? Aren't those flowers beautiful?"

"Well, I…um…" Robert said.

The delivery boy placed a vase of a variety of brightly colored flowers on the counter, then looked at the paper on the clipboard he carried.

"Polly Chapman?" he said.

Polly's head snapped around and her eyes widened as she stared at the gorgeous bouquet. She got to her feet slowly and moved to the counter.

"Those are for me?" she said.

"Yep," the boy said, "if you're Polly Chapman."

"No one has ever sent me flowers before," Polly said, frowning.

"Well, someone has sent you flowers now," Nancy said, beaming. In the next instant she poked Robert on the arm. "Hey, buster, why aren't they for me from you?"

"I knew I was going to be in trouble," Robert muttered, rolling his eyes heavenward. "I just knew it."

Polly signed the paper on the line the boy pointed to, then the messenger left the office, whistling off-key.

Polly buried her nose in the pretty blossoms and inhaled deeply.

"Heavenly," she said. "They smell so good. It's springtime in November."

"Polly, if you don't open the card," Nancy said, "I'm going to blow a fuse in my brain. A woman can take just so much curiosity before something breaks."

"Did it ever occur to you, dear wife," Robert said, "that the identity of Polly's admirer is none of your business?"

"Don't be silly," Nancy said, with a sniff. "Polly is part of our family. Therefore, it's most definitely my business. Polly, the card."

Robert chuckled and shook his head.

Polly pulled the little white envelope free of the plastic, pronged stick and withdrew the card.

"Oh, my," she whispered, feeling a warm flush stain her cheeks.

"Gracious, you're blushing." Nancy peered over Polly's shoulder and read the message on the card aloud.

"'I'm sorry. Dinner? I'll call you. Joe.' Joe? Who's Joe? What's he sorry about?"

"Joe Dillon?" Robert said. "From Abraham Lincoln High School?"

"Well, I…well, yes, I…" Polly stammered.

"What's he sorry about?" Nancy said, frowning. "What did that man do to you that you didn't tell us about?"

"Nothing," Polly said quickly. "We had an argument of sorts over my speech. You know, my telling the students that Jazzy cost thousands of dollars, and his owners were in Europe and…Joe Dillon has some very strong opinions about…some things, that's all."

Like her working for the Dogwoods, Polly thought, and catering to the rich, and on and on and on.

"Oh," Nancy said. "Well, your Joe obviously feels badly about your spat."

"He's not mine," Polly said, the flush on her cheeks deepening.

"Figure of speech," Nancy said. "Is this Joe Dillon good-looking?"

"Scrumptious," Polly said. "What I mean is, he's…he's attractive, in a rugged, earthy, masculine way that… Oh, never mind."

"Interesting," Nancy said. "Very interesting. Joe. Now, there's a strong, no-nonsense name. Yes, very good. I hope he takes you to a snazzy restaurant as part of his apology. What are you going to wear?"

"Nancy," Polly said, "I didn't say that I was going to accept Joe's invitation to dinner."

"Well, why wouldn't you?" Nancy said, raising her eyebrows.

"Because we have such opposite views about certain things that all we would do is argue," she said, slipping the florist card back into the envelope.

And because, she mentally tacked on, she could still remember the startling heat that had swirled within her, then lingered for so long, after Joe's hand had brushed hers.

Because when she looked into those incredible eyes of his, she felt as though she were drowning in their depths.

Because Joe Dillon did tricky little things to her sense of self, made her so acutely aware of her own femininity compared to his blatant masculinity, it was disconcerting, to say the least.

"Then just avoid addressing those issues," Nancy was saying.

"Pardon me?" Polly said, pulling her attention from her jumbled thoughts.

"Goodness, you're spacey," Nancy said. "Joe Dillon has you in a tizzy."

"Oh, he does not," Polly said, frowning. "I don't even like him."

"That's because you got off on the wrong foot with him," Nancy said. "You know, your saying how much Jazzy cost and what have you, during your speech. That's what I was saying. Avoid the topics that you two don't see eye to eye on and enjoy a lovely evening out with a scrumptious...to quote...man."

"I really don't think that's a good idea," Polly said slowly.

"Sure it is," Nancy said. "You're dating a med student and a law student, both of whom are dead broke and exhausted when they surface long enough to take you for pizza, or to a free concert in a park. They're duds."

They're safe! Polly's mind screamed. They were focused on achieving their career goals, had no long-range plans regarding her, simply enjoyed her company when they managed to wiggle a few hours free from their busy schedules.

But Joe Dillon? He was dangerous.

He was the type of man who could render a woman speechless and unable to think clearly.

It wasn't hard to fathom waking up in Joe's bed after a wondrous night of lovemaking and wondering how on earth she had gotten there.

Joe could cause daydreams to become dreams of heartfelt yearning of a home and beautiful baby boys with dark hair and chocolate brown eyes.

Oh, yes, Joe was very, *very* dangerous.

"Polly? Hello?" Nancy said. "You're gone again."

"What? Oh. I was just thinking."

"Well, let's think about what you're going to wear for your dinner date with Joe."

"Nancy," Robert said, smiling, "leave the poor girl alone. Why would Polly want to spend the evening with a man she doesn't even like?"

"Well, in all fairness," Polly said, "that's a rather harsh statement, I guess. I certainly didn't like his attitude about…certain things, and he *was* very grumpy and borderline rude, but I did create a disaster at the assembly, and I suppose that would get on anyone's nerves, because you would not *believe* how noisy and wild those students got in a blink of an eye. Of course, it wasn't my fault, because no one told me what to say, let alone what *not* to say. Then again—am I babbling?"

Nancy and Robert nodded in unison.

Polly sighed. "I thought I was. Look, I need to mull this over. Joe said on the card that he'd call about the dinner date. I'll use the time until then to sift and sort, pro and con, yes and no, and…"

The telephone rang. Polly was so startled by the sudden, shrill sound that she nearly dropped the little white envelope. Robert answered the summons.

"Dogwood Veterinary Clinic," he said cheerfully. "Polly Chapman? Why, yes, she's right here, *Joe.*"

Polly's eyes widened and her heart began to beat in a wild tempo.

"I haven't mulled yet," she whispered frantically to Nancy. "I can't talk to him now. Tell him I died and to call back later."

"No, no, this is better," Nancy said. "You were going to wear out your brain with your mulling. Listen to what Joe has to say, then go with your feminine instincts."

"I think I was absent the day feminine instincts were passed out. I don't have any."

"Of course, you do. You just need to dust them off and use them."

"Polly?" Robert said, extending the receiver toward her.

Polly took the receiver, looked pointedly at Nancy and Robert, then sighed again as she realized they weren't going to budge an inch to allow her some privacy.

"Hello?" she said into the receiver, hoping her voice hadn't really sounded as squawky as Jazzy's.

"Polly? This is Joe Dillon. Did you receive the flowers?"

"Yes, they just arrived and they're very lovely. Thank you."

"Well, I *am* sorry I was so hard on you. Flowers can't erase my behavior, but I hope you'll accept them as my attempt at an apology."

Not fair, not fair, Polly thought. On top of all his other attributes, Joe was now literally oozing gentlemanly charm.

"Yes, of course," she said. "I flew off the handle a

bit myself during our...discussion. That isn't my usual mode of conduct. So, I should apologize to you, too, and I certainly do."

Take that, Joe Dillon, she thought smugly. Tit for tat. A serving of gooey charm given for one received.

"And I accept," Joe said. "We now have a clean slate. I like that. It's the perfect scenario to be in place when we go out to dinner."

"Oh, well, that isn't necessary. I assumed that the dinner invitation was part of soothing ruffled feathers, if Jazzy will excuse the expression, and we've covered the subject of our socially unacceptable behavior."

"Polly," Nancy whispered, "you're blowing it. Treat the dinner as a separate deal."

Polly glared at Nancy.

"No, you're misinterpreting my invitation," Joe said. "It's separate and apart from my apology."

Polly took the receiver from her ear for a second, stared at it, then at a beaming Nancy, as though Nancy and Joe were communicating somehow through the device. She pressed the receiver to her ear again.

"Oh," she said.

"Dinner?" Joe said. "This is Tuesday, so, say Friday night?"

Polly frowned. "Why?"

"So we can get to know each other better in pleasant surroundings instead of a war zone. We'll go somewhere special, have a nice evening together."

"Well..." Polly said slowly.

"Seven-thirty?"

"I suppose it would be..."

"Great. What's your address?"

Polly heard herself rattle off her address, bid Joe a pleasant goodbye, then watched her hand replace the receiver.

"Why did I do that?" she said, ignoring Nancy's cheer of approval. "Why on earth did I do that?"

Why did I do that? Joe thought, staring at the telephone on the end table in his living room. *Why in the hell did I do that?*

He shook his head, glanced at his watch, and got to his feet. He'd sprinted to his house to use the telephone during his lunch hour and needed to get back to the school. He grabbed an apple from a bowl of fruit on the kitchen counter and left the house.

As he strode along the trash-cluttered sidewalk, chomping on the fruit, he knew he was frowning at his actions in regard to Polly Chapman.

All he'd intended to do, he thought, was satisfy his prickling conscious about yelling in Polly's face. Then for reasons he couldn't begin to fathom, he'd added the query "Dinner?" to the florist card.

"Why?" he said aloud, then took another bite of apple.

And if that wasn't confusing enough, he'd talked a mile a minute to convince Polly she should accept his invitation. The apologies on both their parts had been a done deal. The dinner wasn't necessary to mend fences.

Joe tossed the apple core to a mangy-looking dog that gobbled up the treat, tail wagging at full speed.

A knot had twisted in his gut, Joe thought, as he continued on his way, when he'd heard Polly hesitate, declare that the dinner out wasn't needed to sooth ruffled feathers, as she'd put it. Like an adolescent who was besotted by the pretty cheerleader, he'd momentarily panicked over the realization that Polly might actually refuse to go out with him.

"I'm losing it," Joe said aloud, cutting across the parking lot of the school.

Polly Chapman wasn't his type, not even close. His determination to see her again was absurd, ridiculous, didn't make one bit of sense. And equally as baffling was the fact that he couldn't avoid the truth of the knowledge that he was *really* looking forward to his dinner date with Polly on Friday night.

"Weird," he muttered. "Very weird."

"Hey, Coach," a boy yelled, "chirp, chirp, man. You hiding out from that scary bird?"

Joe chuckled and raised one hand in acknowledgment of the hollered razzing.

The kids were having a field day with having witnessed Coach Dillon being bitten on the butt by Jazzy the Killer Macaw, he thought. He was being a good sport about it, as it wasn't every day of the week that students caught an authority figure at an embarrassing disadvantage. He'd let them have their fun until it got boring and they moved on to something else.

But, he thought, a grin breaking across his face, he sure as hell hoped Polly didn't bring that bird along as a bodyguard on their date.

During the remainder of the week, Nancy pestered Polly unmercifully about what Polly was going to wear on her date with Joe Dillon. Polly's continued shrugs caused Nancy to roll her eyes in frustration.

On Friday morning, Nancy cornered Polly as she was cleaning Jazzy's cage.

"You're out of time, Polly Chapman," Nancy said. "Your date is tonight and you still haven't settled on what you're wearing. You should go out on your lunch hour and buy a gorgeous new dress."

"My budget doesn't allow for gorgeous new dresses," Polly said, filling one of Jazzy's water cups.

"Really?" Nancy said. "Aren't we paying you

enough? Goodness, Polly, why didn't you speak up? We'll sit down with Robert and discuss giving you a raise. I mean, heavenly days, everyone's budget should include a chunk for new clothes.''

Polly laughed. ''A chunk? Is that accounting jargon?''

''I'm serious.''

''Nancy,'' Polly said, her smile disappearing as she turned to face her boss, ''you and Robert pay me a very generous salary, and you've given me regular raises. I have no complaints in that department.''

''But?'' Nancy said, frowning. ''Why can't you buy a new dress? I find it hard to believe that you might be a secret gambler, or whatever. Right, Jazzy?''

''Right, Jazzy,'' the bird said, waddling along the table. ''Give me the bird, Joe.''

''Hush, you naughty thing,'' Nancy said. ''Polly?''

Polly sighed. ''It's not complicated, Nancy. You know I have a brother and sister who are twins.''

''Yes, they're freshmen at the U of A.''

''And the University of Arizona is a very expensive place to go to school. Ted and Megan have part-time jobs at a pizza parlor, but it's difficult to work very many hours and keep up your grades. Believe me, I know. I've been there.''

''Can't your parents help out?''

''Oh, they do. Our folks are wonderful, but my mom is a waitress and my dad drives a city bus. There has never been money for a lot of extras. So, I... Well, I stretch my budget to include money for some of Ted's and Megan's expenses.''

''Why didn't I know this?'' Nancy said. ''You've been with us for what...over two years now. You've said you have a close-knit family you adore. That's it. Zip. I didn't have a clue that money was so tight for you.''

Polly shrugged. ''It's not a news bulletin. It's just the

way it is, the way it has always been. That's why I'm a veterinary technician and not a full-fledged veterinarian."

"I see," Nancy said slowly. "I owe you an apology for nagging you about buying a new dress. I had no idea that— I'm sorry."

"Oh, heavens, don't worry about it. Look, I have a peasant skirt and blouse and a pretty shawl I found at a secondhand store a few months ago. I'll wear that tonight. After all, a dinner date with grumpy Joe isn't exactly the happening of the decade. It's no big deal."

Right, Polly thought. She sure wished the butterflies in her stomach would get that message. She'd become increasingly nervous about tonight as the days passed since her telephone conversation with Joe. She just wanted the evening ahead to be over and to be safely back home in her little apartment.

"Well, I hope you have a lovely time tonight," Nancy said. "The outfit you're planning to wear sounds very attractive." She paused. "Do you want some grapes, Jazzy?"

"Grapes," the bird squawked, "and a bottle of beer, Joe."

"Oh, good grief," Polly said, laughing.

Four

That evening, Polly stood in front of the full-length mirror mounted on the back of her bedroom door and resisted the urge to cross her eyes and stick her tongue out at her reflection.

She looked like a gypsy fortune-teller at a carnival, she thought. Really ridiculous. The peasant skirt and blouse and the fringed shawl had seemed like a practical, yet fun, purchase weeks ago. But now? Tonight? As her choice of ensemble for a dinner date with Joe Dillon? The outfit just wouldn't do.

Glancing at her watch, Polly rushed to the closet and swung open the door.

"Oh, darn," she said, with a moan. "Why can't I be Cinderella with a built-in fairy godmother who will zap up a stunning creation for me? I really don't have anything to wear!"

Think, she ordered herself, shoving the hangers past

for her perusal. Improvise. Be artistic. Imaginative. *Something*.

"And hurry up about it, Polly Chapman," she said. "You're running out of time."

Joe entered the courtyard of the apartment complex and glanced around. The one-story structure was in the shape of a horseshoe, with a grassy area in the center. Old-fashioned light posts glowed on the four corners of the grass.

The apartments were small, he mused, checking the numbers as he walked along the sidewalk, and were located in an older section of the middle of the city. It was a well cared for part of town, but there was just so much that could be done to camouflage the ravishes of time.

Strange, Joe thought, stopping in front of Polly's door. He'd expected Polly to live in a bigger and newer building. After all, she was a trained professional who was employed by an uptown veterinarian. Her career and probably subsequent income certainly didn't match her choice of residence.

Well, that statement held true in regard to where he lived, too. But Polly wasn't on the same wavelength he was in regard to that subject, as evidenced by the argument they'd had.

Yes, Polly's choice of residence was strange.

Joe knocked on the door.

Polly jumped to her feet from her perch on the sofa as the sharp rap on the door echoed through the quiet living room. She stood statue still for a moment, willing her racing heart to return to a normal tempo. After taking a deep, steadying breath, she produced a meager smile, then crossed the room to answer the summons at the door.

As Polly appeared in the doorway of the apartment Joe opened his mouth to extend a greeting to her, only to close it again in the next instant when he realized he suddenly had no air in his lungs.

Her hair was a golden halo of soft curls that framed her face, accentuating her delicate features. Her eyes appeared bigger, sparkling like sapphires. Her lips were touched with rosy gloss and beckoned to be kissed.

And, oh, Lord, what she was wearing, Joe thought, stifling a groan as heat rocketed throughout him. Talk about enticingly feminine. The top was a soft hue of rose silk with narrow straps and row upon row of tiny pleats covering her breasts.

It had a name, that sinful creation. He'd seen a picture of one in a magazine. It was…yes, a camisole, a sexy, drive-a-man-over-the-edge camisole.

Polly had tucked it into black slacks that hugged the womanly slope of her hips to perfection and had added high heel shoes, which made her slender legs seem to go on forever.

Oh, man, he was dying, right there on the minuscule square of cement in front of Polly's weather-beaten front door.

"Joe?" Polly said.

"Huh?" He cleared his throat. "Yes, hello. Good evening. How are you? You look…you look sensational, Polly."

"Well, thank you," she said, with a little dip of her head. "Would you like to come in?"

"Certainly." Joe stepped into the living room and Polly closed the door behind him, slowly, very slowly, attempting to buy time to recover from the shattering impact of Joe Dillon.

Joe Dillon, so gorgeous in a tan suit and tie, with a dark brown shirt that was the exact color of his fudge-sauce eyes. Joe, with shoulders as wide as Toledo in the obviously custom-tailored suit. Joe, with his thick, shaggy, dark brown hair that caused her fingertips to tingle at the fleeting, enticing thought of sinking them into those gleaming strands.

Oh, dear heaven, her bones were dissolving.

"Nice place," Joe said, glancing around. But so damn small and shabby, despite Polly's immaculate house-keeping. Why did she live here? "Very nice."

"I like it," she said, turning to face him. "It's cozy. Even more, it's mine. My very first apartment."

"Then you lived at home while you were attending college?"

"Oh, my, yes. My twin brother and sister are at home, too, and they're freshmen at the U of A. My parents are so proud that all three of their children will have gone to college."

Joe nodded. "As well they should be. Do both of your parents work?"

"Yes. Why?"

"No reason." Joe shrugged. "I'm just chatting. Are you ready to go? I made reservations."

"Yes. I'll just get my purse and…and shawl."

Polly hurried across the room and into the bedroom, making certain she stepped out of Joe's view when she entered the room.

Pressing one hand on her stomach, she drew a steadying breath.

She looked sensational, Joe had said, she thought, swallowing a bubble of laughter. She was actually getting away with this. She'd seen the raw, male approval of her attire reflected in Joe's expressive eyes.

He didn't have a clue that she was actually wearing a fancy slip her aunt had sent her for Christmas. She'd whacked off the bottom with a pair of scissors and there she was, a braless wonder, knocking the socks off worldly Joe Dillon. What a hoot.

Polly picked up a piece of pale pink lacy material and settled it around her shoulders, aware it was useless as a barrier against the chilly evening air.

But, oh, well, it completed her odd outfit to perfection. She only hoped that Joe didn't ask to use her bathroom, where he might notice that there was no curtain on the window. The curtain was going out to dinner with Mr. Dillon.

As Polly and Joe walked along the sidewalk edging the courtyard in her apartment complex, he told her he'd made reservations at a restaurant that was nestled at the base of the Catalina Mountains on the far northwest side of town.

Polly nodded but said nothing as she recognized the name of the establishment as one of Tucson's most exclusive places to dine, and one she certainly had never been to. She smiled to herself, glad she had changed her attire from her gypsy outfit to the smashing creation she now wore.

The car that Joe assisted Polly into was a dark blue, sleek sports model that was obviously very new.

Polly wiggled further into the butter-soft bucket seat and inhaled the pleasant aroma of rich leather.

"It smells so nice in here," she said, as Joe drove away from the curb.

Joe laughed. "That's it? My car *smells* good? Haven't

you read the magazine articles that say a man's vehicle is his most prized possession, his favorite toy, and that he expects a woman to gush profusely about it?''

"No, I guess I missed those very important instructions." Polly smiled. "I'm more inclined to wonder whether you're worried about a car like this one being stolen in the neighborhood where you live."

"I rent a garage behind a service station a few blocks from my place. Oh, and for the record…I'm not bonkers over this vehicle. I simply like to drive something with enough power to allow me to hold my own in heavy traffic." Joe paused. "The streets of Tucson are getting very congested as time goes by. Don't you get nervous driving that van of yours?''

Polly shrugged. "Not really. It gets me where I'm going…eventually. My father and brother keep my van in as good a condition as is possible. There's no sense in fussing over something I can't do anything about."

Joe glanced at Polly, then quickly redirected his attention to the traffic.

"You have a very *accepting*…for the lack of a better word…attitude about things, don't you?''

Polly laughed. The lilting resonance caused a coil of heat to twist low in Joe's body and he shifted slightly in his seat, frowning in the process.

"That's a polite way to put it," Polly said, still smiling. "I've been accused of being a Pollyanna ad nauseum. My brother once told me that my given name didn't give me license to go nuts, and that if I said, 'Look at the bright side' once more, he was definitely going to erase me from this world."

Joe chuckled. Polly slid him a glare he didn't see, mentally telling him that the sexy sound should be declared against the law and he'd better knock it off.

"Being a Pollyanna Polly isn't all bad," he said, "as long as you keep that frame of mind in its proper perspective."

"Meaning?"

"Well, if it's too automatic," Joe continued, "you could give up, accept things as they are, live with the status quo, before you really have to. You might actually have more, do more, if you tried."

"That's a reasonable theory, I suppose, but it doesn't apply to me."

"Doesn't it?" Joe said quietly.

"If you're attempting to make a point, Mr. Dillon," Polly said, a slight edge to her voice, "I'm missing it. Why don't you just spell out what it is you're attempting to say?"

Joe sighed. "I'm sorry. We're headed for a collision course again—an argument waiting to erupt. Forget what I said." He cleared his throat. "So, Ms. Chapman, did you notice how the stars are twinkling like a million diamonds in the black velvet sky tonight? Very pretty. Very nice. The *bright side* to look at right now is heavenward."

Polly's intention to pursue the veiled comment Joe had made, press for an explanation, was pushed aside by his delightful change of subject.

The sky, she thought, *was* a spectacle of beauty, picture-perfect. She didn't want to argue with Joe again. She was on the way to a fabulous restaurant in the company of an extremely handsome man. She felt lovely and feminine in her daring attire, and would hold her own in the elegant atmosphere.

This, Polly decided, was like a Cinderella night, as though a fairy godmother really had appeared with a magical wand in hand.

No, she didn't intend to squabble with Joe. She was going to enjoy, savor, every minute of the hours ahead, knowing she was stepping into a world where she'd never been, nor probably would ever go to again.

During the drive to the restaurant, Polly and Joe chatted comfortably about the weather, the U of A and Phoenix Suns basketball teams, and a bestselling book that was about to be released as a movie.

With each passing mile, Polly became more relaxed, allowing the mystical image in her mind of being Cinderella in a fairy-tale land to settle over her completely, like a soft, snugly blanket.

Yet, intermingled with the contentment was an ever growing sense of excitement and anticipation about what the magical night ahead might bring.

It was as though, she thought dreamily, as Joe turned into the parking lot of the restaurant, she were floating above herself, watching from afar like a fascinated observer.

After giving the car keys to a valet, Joe escorted a smiling Polly into the building, where they were greeted immediately by a hostess. Minutes later they were seated at a cloth-covered table with a small candle in the center, glowing in a china holder.

A tuxedo-clad waiter appeared, gave them oversize menus and announced he would return shortly.

As Joe studied the dinner selections, Polly took inventory of the large room.

Enchanting, she thought. Everything was so beautiful, so special. There were sparkling, crystal chandeliers hanging from the ceiling, the tables were arranged to allow for private conversations, the diners were dressed in exquisite finery.

There was an aura of make-believe about it all, like a movie set where everyone had been put in place to perform a role of elegance.

But that made sense, Polly mused. This was, indeed, a Cinderella fairy-tale night, and the most minute detail had been attended to with precise perfection.

Joe set his menu to one side on the table, folded his arms over his chest and looked at Polly.

There was, he thought, knowing he was smiling, a delightful and refreshing childlike expression on Polly's face. Her incredible blue eyes were sweeping the room, and he could tell she was cataloging, memorizing, all that she saw.

Polly had not, he was certain, ever been to a restaurant that was this classy and expensive, with the trappings that went with the ridiculously high prices on the menu.

Why? Surely she dated, was sought after by the male populace of Tucson. Why hadn't some man wined and dined her, taken her to places like this one, to symphonies and live theater performances? It was as though by bringing her here, he was introducing her to a world she'd never experienced before.

And he felt about ten feet tall.

He was Prince Charming, riding up on his mighty white horse to scoop Cinderella from the dusty hearth where she labored, and whisk her away to the land of enchantment.

Joe frowned.

Lord, he thought, where had all that malarkey come from? Cinderella? Prince Charming? They were characters from a fairy tale, were make-believe, were not remotely close to reality.

And he, Joe Dillon, dealt solely in reality.

The waiter reappeared at the table.

"Polly?" Joe said. "Have you decided what you'd like to have for dinner?"

"Hmm?" She shifted her gaze slowly to Joe. She blinked. "Oh. Goodness, I'm terribly sorry. I haven't even looked at the menu. I'll just have whatever you've selected."

"Are you sure? You can take as much time as you need to decide."

"No, no, your choice will be fine. This poor man has enough to do, without having to come back to our table to get my order."

Joe shrugged, selected a wine, then requested dinners of prime rib, baked potatoes and salad to be served with the meal. Polly spread the mint green linen napkin on her lap, smoothing it into exacting place.

This pretty napkin, she thought, frowning slightly, was made of material finer than any tablecloth her mother had ever owned.

No matter how exhausted her mom had been after hours on her feet waitressing at the busy café, she'd always set a pretty table for her family's evening meal. How thrilled she would be to have linen napkins like this one.

"Polly?" Joe said, as the waiter hurried away. "Are you all right?"

Polly's head snapped up and she smiled. "Oh, yes, I'm fine. I was just admiring this beautiful napkin."

Joe frowned. "The napkin?"

"The material is lovely and it has a tiny, rolled type of hem that has a fancy name that I can't remember. Don't you think they're a gorgeous shade of green? The color coordinates perfectly with all the other accents in the room."

Joe crossed his arms on the table and leaned slightly toward Polly.

"You're serious, aren't you?" he said.

"Pardon me?" Polly said, obviously confused by his question.

"You're sitting there sincerely marveling over the quality, the color, the hem, for Pete's sake, of a table napkin."

Polly lifted her chin. "I happen to believe that the napkins are…"

"Wait," Joe said, straightening and raising one hand. "I wasn't making fun of you, Polly, or belittling you in any way. Your obviously genuine delight in that napkin is extremely refreshing, it really is."

"Oh." Her flash of anger disappeared as quickly as it had come.

"I've never met anyone like you before," Joe said, looking directly into Polly's blue eyes. "That's a compliment, not a put-down. I've eaten in this restaurant on many occasions, and I've never taken the time to appreciate the pretty napkins." He glanced around, then looked at her again. "Or anything else, for that matter." He nodded. "This is a nice place, isn't it?"

"It's beautiful," Polly said, hardly above a whisper. "It's like a color picture in a magazine, or a scene in a movie."

Dear heaven, she thought, she couldn't breathe, and her heart was beating so wildly she could hear the thundering tempo echoing in her ears. She was pinned in place by Joe's eyes, those mesmerizing eyes.

Heat was beginning to thrum low in her body. That was desire in its purest form. How feminine and alive she felt, so aware of her womanliness and Joe's incredible manliness.

Polly pulled her gaze from Joe's and smoothed the napkin yet again on her lap.

Oh, dear, dear, she thought, she was treading in such foreign and dangerous waters. It was as though she were being swept away by the raging, sensual current of those waters, being overwhelmed by the blatant, masculine magnetism of Joe Dillon.

She was so out of her league it was a crime, Polly thought dismally. She wasn't worldly, or sophisticated enough, to be in the company of a man like Joe. She didn't belong in this fancy restaurant, playing dress-up in a cutoff slip and a bathroom curtain.

What would be expected of her in this environment? Did dinner out with meal prices almost equal to her entire weekly food budget mean she was to understand that the evening would end with going to bed with the man who had picked up the check?

Well, ha! No way. That wasn't how she operated, wasn't remotely close to her set of values. She was going to make that very clear to sexy Mr. Dillon right now, so she wouldn't have to stew about it all evening and ruin her Cinderella night on the town.

Polly raised her eyes to look at Joe, not seeing the wine steward approaching the table.

"I want you to know," she said, hoping her voice wasn't as wobbly as it sounded to her own ears, "that if you're assuming that I'm going to go to bed..."

"Your bed, sir," the wine steward said, then cleared his throat. "That is, your wine, sir."

Polly plunked one elbow on the table and rested her forehead on her palm.

"Oh, good grief," she said, feeling the hot flush of embarrassment on her cheeks. "I don't believe this."

Joe stared at Polly with wide eyes, looked at the bottle of wine, then back at Polly.

"Sir?" the steward said.

"What?" Joe said. "Yes, that's fine. Forget the tasting ritual. Just pour it."

"Very good, sir."

The steward filled their glasses halfway, placed the bottle on the table, then succumbed to a burst of laughter he could no longer contain. "Enjoy your evening."

"Right," Joe said, glaring at him.

As the grinning man hurried away, Joe reached across the table and jiggled Polly's arm.

"Hello?" he said. "Are you there?"

"No," she said, not moving. "I'm not here. I'm at home, alone, curled up with a book. I did *not* just make a complete fool of myself in the fanciest restaurant I've ever been to in my entire life. Go away."

Joe smiled and a strange warmth suffused him with a gentle touch like nothing he'd experienced before.

Polly, Polly, he thought. She was like a breath of fresh, spring air, so real, so honest. He'd been on the mark when he'd surmised that she didn't move in the fast lane of upscale restaurants and the swinging singles scene.

It was as though Polly Chapman were of another time and place, and he'd transported her to a world where she was afraid she didn't know the rules of conduct.

He'd bet twenty bucks that she'd been about to tell him in no uncertain terms that taking her to a pricey restaurant wouldn't automatically gain him access to her bed.

Ah, Polly, sweet Polly. He felt so protective of her, wanted to scoop her up and reassure her that he would never ask more of her than she was willing to give, never make demands of her, nor frighten her.

She was like…yes, a hummingbird, Joe mused on. So fragile, delicate, yet possessing inner strength of survival and determination. She was really something, this Polly Chapman. Very special. Very rare. Very lovely.

Dillon, he thought, cutting off his rambling thoughts, *get it together.* What he said to Polly in the next few minutes could mean the difference between an evening that was now a disaster in her opinion, and one that was the stuff of which fond memories were made.

Oh, cripes, where had that poetic nonsense come from? He had to talk to Polly before she crawled under the table and refused to budge.

"Polly, look at me."

"No."

"Please?"

Polly sighed and raised her head, dropping her hands to her lap. The expression on her face was a study in misery, and Joe's heart thudded painfully in his chest.

"Forget what happened with the wine steward," he said, smiling at her gently. "I think I know what you were attempting to say. We're going to enjoy our meal, these hours together, then I'll walk you to your door and bid you good-night. Okay?"

"Yes." Polly sighed again. "I apologize if I embarrassed you in front of the man with the wine. You must think I'm such a child, an unsophisticated…"

"Lovely, refreshing, delightful woman," Joe concluded. He picked up his wineglass. "Shall we make a toast to the remainder of a splendid evening?"

Polly hesitated a moment, the lifted her glass.

"All right," she said, smiling. "Thank you, Joe. Thank you very much."

They took a sip of wine, gazes still meeting over the tops of the wafer-thin glasses. It was a special moment, a moment of acceptance, trust and greater understanding. And it was a moment of desire humming, glowing hotter, pulsing.

The sensual spell was broken by the waiter appearing at the table. He flipped open a stand, then settled a heavy tray on top. He then placed the plates of food on the table, reciting what each of the diners was receiving.

Joe chuckled as the man bustled away with the portable stand.

"Did you ever think about how ridiculous that ritual is?" he said, smiling. "It's as though we just landed here from another planet and have no idea what this lumpy thing is, so the guy tells us it's a baked potato. The whole number is weird."

Polly nodded and picked up her fork.

Just landed here from another planet, she mentally repeated. That about summed it up…the way she felt being in this restaurant with Joe Dillon.

Well, okay, she'd go with that fanciful theory. She was exploring new territory in the form of a high-society eating establishment, and the close proximity of a man like none she'd ever encountered before.

And when in doubt? Wing it.

Because of Joe's class act manner in which he'd handled her mortifying behavior, the slate was wiped clean, allowing the hours left in the evening to be savored, enjoyed. And she intended to do exactly that.

Polly took a bite of fluffy potato.

"Mmm—delicious." She paused. "When I was at the high school, the students called you Coach. What sport are you connected with?"

"Basketball," Joe said, cutting into his prime rib.

"The season has officially begun, and we've won our first four games."

"Really? That's fantastic. You must be an excellent coach."

Joe shrugged. "I manage to get the job done. The truth of the matter is, there is incredible talent waiting to be tapped, trained, in that school. Do you have any idea what channeling that ability, that energy, could mean for those boys, Polly?"

"Well, I…"

"If I can reach them," Joe continued in a rush, "make them believe in themselves, help them become dedicated athletes, there's a fighting chance they'll stay off the streets, actually say no to drugs and gang influence.

"For a few, it might be a ticket out of the ghetto with a college athletic scholarship. I've seen it happen in the ten years I've been at Lincoln, and it can and will happen again. I…"

Joe stopped speaking and cleared his throat.

"Sorry," he said. "I was off and running on my soap box."

"No, don't apologize. You care deeply about what you're doing, about those kids. I think that's wonderful, and they're very fortunate to have you in their corner. It's just that… Never mind."

Joe frowned slightly as he took a bite of meat, chewed and swallowed.

"Just that…what?" he said.

"Oh, dear, dear," Polly said, "I'm overstepping. It's none of my business, but it just seems to me that you're giving everything, all of you, to those students. You even live in the ghetto to be, as you said, able to better relate to them."

"So?" he said, his frown deepening.

"What about you, the man, the person? Don't you have hopes, dreams, wants and needs? Don't you yearn for a family, a wife and babies? A nice home where your own children can grow up?"

"No," he said gruffly. "I'm perfectly fine, contented, fulfilled, with my life exactly the way it's presently structured."

"If you say so," Polly said, with a little shrug.

"I say so," Joe said, then stabbed another piece of meat with more force than necessary. "It sure as hell beats baby-sitting pampered birds that go around biting people on the butt."

"Now wait just a minute here," Polly said, her voice rising. "We're discussing *your* career and life-style choices, not mine. I..."

"Joe Dillon," a woman's voice sang out. "Darling, it has been ages since I've seen you."

Polly's and Joe's heads snapped up to see a stunning woman in her early thirties advancing toward them. She was wearing an elegant, full-length white evening gown and had a fur wrap draped lazily over one shoulder.

Oh, hell, Joe thought.

Oh, my goodness, Polly thought.

Joe got to his feet and received an air-kiss near his right cheek delivered by the beaming beauty.

"Hello, Celine," he said. "I'd like you to meet Polly Chapman."

"Charmed," Celine said, glancing quickly at Polly, then redirecting her full attention to Joe. "You naughty devil, you've been hiding again. What is it going to take to drag you out of your dreary little world?"

"Celine..." Joe said.

"I saw your parents at the Governor's Ball, where you were glaringly absent," Celine babbled on, "and they said you're hopeless. Darling, there are a whole bunch of us flying to Aspen in Ricky's plane to ski between Christmas and New Year's. Say you'll come. You've been before, and you know what fun we have.''

"Look, Celine, I'm not—"

"Don't say no," Celine said, pouting prettily. "Just think about it. Oh, I must tell you that Buffy is still enjoying your yacht to the max. I can't imagine why you ever sold it, but she adores it. I must dash. Lunch soon? At the country club? Bye, darling. It was nice meeting you, Molly.''

"Polly," she said absently, her mind racing.

Skiing in Aspen, having flown there in someone's private plane? she thought. The Governor's Ball? People named Ricky and Buffy? A yacht? Lunch at the country club?

Was this crazy?

Everything that darling Celine had gushed added up to a very startling fact.

Joe Dillon was a jet-set dropout.

Joe Dillon was, apparently, a very wealthy man.

Five

Joe sank back onto his chair, feeling as though he'd just gone ten rounds in a boxing ring. He was drained, not only from Celine's unexpected appearance, then nonstop blather, but also because he realized that Polly had heard every word spoken and had, therefore, gathered information about him that he'd had no intention of divulging.

Damn, he thought, pulling the knot of his suddenly too tight tie down a half an inch. This evening was now definitely shot to hell. Polly would hammer him with questions, he'd become angry and defensive, and a lousy time would be had by all.

Slowly and very reluctantly, Joe shifted his gaze to Polly, fully expecting her to be ready to pounce. To his wide-eyed amazement, she was poking around in her salad bowl with her fork, as though searching for hidden treasure.

"Polly?" Joe said tentatively.

"Hmm?" she said, not looking up as she pushed aside a cherry tomato.

"I imagine you're curious about some of the things that Celine said."

"Ah, there it is," Polly said. "I knew I'd seen a chunk of radish in here."

She speared it with her fork, then popped it into her mouth, nodding in approval as she chewed and swallowed.

"I love radishes," she said. "They're so crisp and crunchy. My mother knows how to make radishes look like flowers by cutting them a special way, but I've never been able to get the hang of it."

"Polly," Joe said, frowning as he leaned slightly toward her. "Celine?"

"Celine? Oh, well, she was very beautiful, and her dress and fur probably cost more than I make in a year. I did not, however, appreciate her calling me Molly, instead of Polly. Being gorgeous doesn't excuse a person from having proper social manners. I mean, it's not as though Polly is a difficult name to remember. One would think that Celine could have…"

"Would you cut it out?" Joe said, then glanced around quickly and lowered his voice when he spoke again. "We're not discussing how much Celine's dress cost or how bad her manners are."

"Why are we discussing her at all?" Polly said. "You were spotted by an old friend, she turned into Miss Chatter-Cheeks of America, then off she went. End of story. If there's more to talk about regarding her, you're going to have to give me a hint as to what it is."

"You're kidding," Joe said, sinking back in his chair. "Don't you have a million questions to fling at me?"

"Well," Polly said slowly, "there is one thing I'm wondering about."

"I knew it. Here we go."

"Joe, did a mother actually gaze lovingly at her new-born daughter and announce that she was naming her baby Buffy?"

"Damn it, Polly," Joe said, "let's cut to the chase. I'm rich. Okay? My family has so much money it's ridiculous. I was raised by parents who believe that all problems can be solved by cold, hard cash. They don't listen, don't hear, they just whip out the checkbook and ask how much you need to fix whatever is bothering you."

"I'm so sorry," Polly said softly.

"Hey, I admittedly liked the megabucks when I was a teenager," Joe continued, as though Polly hadn't spoken. "I had a fancy car, huge wardrobe, a state-of-the-art stereo system, the whole nine yards.

"I'd long since learned how to deal with my own problems and concerns. I knew my parents loved me. They just didn't know how to deal with me other than on an adult level from the time I was a little kid."

"Oh, dear, dear," Polly said, frowning.

"I went with the program, announcing when I enrolled in college that I would become an attorney like my father. I became engaged to a debutante, a friend of Celine's, who was of our…quote…social standing. Then…"

Joe stopped speaking and stared into memory-filled space. Polly looked at him intently, her heart aching for the lonely little boy Joe must have been. She could envision him so clearly in her mind, surrounded by every toy imaginable, but having no one to talk to, share with, no one to give him a hug.

"Then one summer," Joe continued, pulling Polly from her thoughts, "I volunteered, on impulse, to coach an inner-city basketball team, and everything changed. Everything. I was suddenly existing in a world I'd been vaguely aware of, but hadn't paid one bit of attention to. The months I spent in the ghetto with those kids was reality, the way things really were."

That wasn't entirely true, Polly thought. Joe seemed to be viewing it all in black and white, with people being either very rich, or very poor. It was as though he'd erased the middle-class, the center-section of society.

"There was no stopping me then," Joe said. "I changed my major to education. My parents bellowed their rage, and my fiancée broke our engagement, saying she had no intention of living on a teacher's salary. I've never been sorry for the decision I made."

Joe sighed and shook his head.

"Even after all these years my parents are convinced I'll come to my senses any minute now. They're on my case about it all the time. I try not to lose my temper when I'm with them, because they're the only parents I have.

"On occasion I attend some fancy function with them to please them. Whenever I do that, I run into someone like Celine, who immediately believes I'm back where I belong. I— Hell."

"Hell?" Polly said. "Hell what?"

"I've never spilled out all this garbage to anyone before," Joe said, his dark brows knitted in a frown. "Why did I just dump all of that on you?"

"Maybe because I was listening to you, Joe," Polly said quietly. "Really hearing what you were saying."

Joe looked directly into Polly's blue eyes.

"Yes," he said, "I guess that's why. You're a good

listener, Polly. I feel like a jerk for pouring out my life story but... Well, thank you." He paused. "Can we still salvage the rest of this evening together?"

"Certainly," Polly said, smiling. "I'll dive back into my salad and see if I can find another radish."

This was not the time, nor the place, she thought, to get into a heavy debate with Joe about his life-style, to point out that he'd gone to extremes, in her opinion, to make his stand clear to his parents and former friends. It wouldn't take much at the moment to make Joe erupt like an angry volcano.

Joe tackled the remainder of his now cold dinner, realizing he had lost his appetite as he forced himself to chew and swallow bite after bite.

Lord, he thought in self-disgust, what had come over him? It was as though Polly had slipped a nickel into some hidden slot in his head, causing him to talk until he was blue in the face, tell her things that were buried deep within him.

And the really disturbing thing was that he felt better for it. It had been somehow freeing to unburden himself, to speak of the ongoing frustration he experienced when dealing with his parents, and the friends from another and past era of his life, to spell out his etched-in-stone convictions of why he'd chosen the life-style he led.

Polly had listened to him, really heard what he'd said, passing no censure. That, he supposed, was what was known as sharing...and caring. It was nice, very, very nice.

It did not, however, explain why he had done it. What strange spell was this refreshing, lovely, Pollyanna Polly of a woman weaving around him?

You'd better watch your step, Dillon, he told himself.

He usually had his guard up automatically when he was in the company of a woman from the singles scene.

But with Polly? She was so open and honest, so far removed from the social set he was accustomed to. He found himself relaxing, just being himself, Joe Dillon, exactly as he was.

Oh, yeah, he most definitely had better watch his step in regard to Polly Chapman. He was treading on foreign turf, where there was the danger lurking in the shadows of losing his heart before he knew what hit him.

And that wasn't going to happen. No way. No how.

They finished their dinners accompanied by comfortable silences and idle chitchat that continued on through coffee with brandy served in snifters that caught the glow of the light from the dwindling candle on the table.

Too soon, too soon, Polly thought, as they left the restaurant and were driving toward her apartment. She didn't want her Cinderella night to be over yet.

Her daring camisole top would turn back into a cutoff slip, and her shawl would once again be a bathroom curtain. She would be Polly Chapman, who catered to pampered macaws and poodles with meals delivered from gourmet cooks. How depressing.

No, no, that wasn't right, wasn't how she felt about her job, her career. There was far more in her day than Jazzy the macaw and Pookie the poodle. She was a certified veterinary technician, with responsibilities and tasks befitting her degree. She was happy and fulfilled, a useful and important part of the team at Dogwood Veterinary Clinic.

Polly slid a glance at Joe as he concentrated on maneuvering through the heavy traffic.

It was all Joe's fault that she'd suddenly had bleak

thoughts about her work, she mused, drinking in the sight of Joe's rugged profile that was clearly visible in the city lights. He had made it clear that he believed she was selling out, wasn't giving back to the portion of society she'd come from.

That was so narrow-minded of Joe Dillon, so rotten and stubborn and...

Oh, Polly, stop it, she scolded herself. She was going to get herself into an angry tizzy and ruin the ending of this magical night.

It didn't matter what Joe Dillon thought, because she'd probably never see him again. He was accustomed to being with women like Celine, for heaven's sake. No, she wouldn't hear from Joe after tonight, so she was going to enjoy and savor the remaining time until they said goodbye.

"Yes," she said, with a decisive nod.

Joe looked over at Polly quickly, then redirected his attention to his driving.

"Yes...what?" he said.

"Oh, I didn't realize I had spoken aloud. I was just thinking about something."

"Mmm," he said, chuckling. "Am I allowed to apply that yes to any question I now choose?"

Polly laughed. "Absolutely not."

"Well, hell," Joe said, snapping his fingers.

"Sorry, Coach, but you can't win them all." Polly paused. "Although I do wish you luck in winning the majority of your basketball games during the season. You certainly have a wonderful start."

"We do, indeed," Joe said, parking next to the curb in front of Polly's apartment complex.

Joe came around and assisted Polly from the car. They

walked slowly toward her apartment, Joe encircling her shoulders with one arm and tucking her close to his side.

"I had a lovely time, Joe," Polly said quietly. "Thank you."

"I thank *you*," he said. "It was a very special evening." They stopped in front of her door. "Your key?"

Polly produced the key, Joe unlocked the door, then pushed it open. They stood in the semidarkness, a faint glow from the post light falling over them.

"I was just wondering," Joe said, "if you'd like to see my boys in action. I wouldn't ask you drive down to Lincoln alone, but tomorrow night we play at Copper High School on this side of town. Are you interested?"

"I'd love it," Polly said, smiling. "What time?"

"Tip-off is at eight o'clock. I can't pick you up because I have to stay with the team."

"That's fine. I'll be there, and I'm already looking forward to it."

Joe cradled her face in his large hands.

"Good," he said, lowering his head toward hers. "That's very good."

He brushed his lips over Polly's in a feathery caress that sent shivers coursing down her spine. In the next instant he captured her lips in a searing kiss that seemed to steal the very breath from her body.

Polly's arms floated upward to wrap around Joe's neck as he dropped his hands to her back to nestle her against his body.

The kiss was ecstasy. It was desire thrumming, then coiling, low and hot in a body femininely soft and one masculinely rugged. The kiss tasted of lingering, rich brandy.

Polly's breasts were crushed with an enticing, sensual

pain to the hard wall of Joe's chest, as she returned the hungry kiss in total abandon.

She was hurled back into the sensuous, misty woods with the glittering, silver trees. She was dancing with Joe and now, *at last,* he was kissing her as they swayed to the beautiful music.

She'd waited an eternity for this kiss and it was all, and more, that her dream in the night had promised it would be.

This kiss and the waltz, she thought hazily, should never end.

Joe raised his head a fraction of an inch to draw a rough breath, then slanted his mouth in the opposite direction, claiming Polly's lips once more.

Polly, his mind thundered. The hours spent with her had been fantastic, unbelievable, so real and open and honest. She'd constantly surprised and delighted him with her unexpected reactions and hint of vulnerability and innocence.

She was fresh air and sunshine, and down-to-earth goodness, accompanied by a womanly passion that was sending him up in flames.

Polly was unique, so special and rare, like no woman he had met before.

And he wanted her with an intensity that was beyond anything he had experienced.

Along with the burning need, Joe knew, were emotions of protectiveness, possessiveness and the fierce determination to stand between her and anything that would dim her bright glow, her ability to always see the light in the darkness.

Joe ended the kiss slowly and reluctantly.

"Polly," he murmured, close to her lips, "I promised

to walk you to your door and say good-night. Remember?''

''Hmm?'' she said, gazing at him through her lashes.

Joe gripped her shoulders and eased her away from his aroused body.

''I've got to keep that promise,'' he said, then drew a shuddering breath. ''It's important that I do. *Very* important.''

''It is?'' Polly blinked, then snapped to attention. ''Oh. Oh, my. Yes, of course it is.'' She frowned. ''Why is it *very* important?''

Joe smiled. ''Because I always keep my promises.''

''That makes sense.''

''But it's more than that.'' Joe's smile faded and he drew his thumb gently over Polly's moist lips, causing her to shiver from the sensuous sensation. ''You had a preconceived notion that I would try to hustle you into bed after taking you to an expensive restaurant. I don't want to do anything remotely close to making you believe that's true. Understand?''

''Yes,'' she said, smiling warmly, ''and thank you.''

''Mmm,'' he said nodding, then laughed. ''I deserve a good conduct medal for this. You've turned me inside out, Ms. Chapman.'' He sobered. ''I do want you, Polly, but I'm sure you realize that.''

''I...''

''Shh,'' he said, then dropped a quick kiss onto her lips. ''I'll see you tomorrow night at the game.''

''Yes,'' Polly whispered.

''Good night, Polly.''

She nodded and entered her apartment, closing the door with a quiet click. Joe waited until he heard the lock snap into place, then started back down the sidewalk.

Whew, he thought. That delicate little hummingbird packed a potent, sexual punch. The taste and feel of Polly's lips, the sensation of having her slender body pressed to his, had caused instant flames of desire to rocket throughout him.

Oh, yes, he wanted Polly Chapman.

He was burning with the want of her.

Joe settled behind the wheel of his car, but didn't turn the key in the ignition.

Why? he asked himself. Why had he urged Polly to attend tomorrow night's game? And why had he experienced such a rush of relief and…okay, he'd admit it…joy, when Polly had agreed to come? And why had it been so important that Polly thought well of him, knew he could be trusted to keep his promises?

Damn it, he thought, turning the key in the ignition with more force than was necessary. What was Polly Chapman doing to him?

Oh, dear, dear, Polly thought, as she finished hanging the bathroom curtain in its proper place. Why had she agreed to go to that basketball game tomorrow night? She'd just opened her mouth and out popped "I'd love to. What time?" before she'd even known she was going to speak.

Polly sighed, gave the curtain an appreciative little pat for performing so well in its new role all evening, then she began to prepare for bed.

When she slipped beneath the sheet and blanket, she turned off the small lamp on the nightstand, then stared up at a ceiling she knew was there, but wasn't visible in the darkness.

She had truly believed that she wouldn't see Joe again after tonight. But now? She was going to see him to-

morrow night. Was that a good idea? Or was she fool-
ishly treading further and further into dangerous, un-
known territory?

Polly placed the fingertips of one hand lightly on her
lips, remembering, savoring, the exquisite kiss shared
with Joe.

Never before, *never,* had she been consumed by such
instantaneous, heated desire. She had wanted Joe Dillon,
had wanted to make sweet, beautiful love with him
through the hours of the night.

"Oh, dear, dear," Polly said aloud.

She rolled onto her stomach, punched her pillow into
a marshmallow-soft ball and willed herself to give way
to the escape of slumber.

But blissful sleep was a long time in coming.

"Watch their feet, Ref," Polly yelled. "They're traveling so much they've packed their suitcases!"

A pretty girl sitting next to a standing Polly tugged
on the back of her sweatshirt.

"You'd better sit your butt down, Bird Lady," the
girl said, "or you're going to get us tossed right out of
this gym."

"Oh, sorry." Polly plunked her bottom on the wooden
bleachers. "But did you see that, Debbie?" Polly said
to her new, young acquaintance. "Those referees have
to be blind. Oh-h-h, it makes me so mad I could just
spit."

The boy sitting on the other side of Polly laughed.

"Don't spit, either," he said, "or you'll really get us
tossed."

"All right, all right," Polly said, raising both hands.
"I'm calm. Under control. I'll behave like a mature
adult. You two were very nice to let me sit with you,

and I won't embarrass you again.'' She paused. ''I hope.''

Debbie laughed. ''You're okay, you know that? For being an older person and all, you're fun, you're cool.''

''Thanks,'' Polly said, frowning slightly. ''I think.''

''So,'' the boy said, ''the Bird Lady is now Coach Dillon's lady. That's cool. Works for me.''

''Oh, well, Jerome,'' Polly said, feeling a flush of heat on her cheeks, ''I'm not Coach Dillon's lady, per se. He simply invited me to watch his team play. We'd been out to dinner, you see, and he suddenly suggested that I might like to— Never mind.''

''You're his lady,'' Debbie said, nodding decisively. ''If I were you, though, I wouldn't settle for that dinky little house Coach Dillon lives in by Lincoln. No way. When Jerome and I get married we're leaving that neighborhood so fast you won't see our behinds disappearing. Doesn't make any sense that Coach Dillon lives down there.''

''It doesn't?'' Polly said, her eyes widening as she stared at Debbie.

''Hell, no,'' Jerome said. Polly snapped her head around to look at him. ''If I had the big bucks a teacher makes, I'd find me a fine house uptown to take Debbie to. Nobody gets the drift on why Coach Dillon keeps on hanging his hat in the ghetto.''

''Have you ever said this to him?'' Polly said.

''No way,'' Jerome said. ''Where we come from, you don't mess in anyone's business. You know what I mean?''

''Well, his lady can mess in his business, Jerome,'' Debbie said.

''True,'' Jerome said, smiling. ''You mess in my business big-time, girl.''

"You've got that straight, my man," Debbie said, "and you'd do well to remember it. Hey, we got two more points. Way to go, Luis. Clean their clocks."

Polly redirected her attention to the fast-moving game, then slid a glance at Joe. From where she was sitting with Debbie and Jerome, she could see Joe in profile.

He was leaning forward, his eyes riveted on the players. His elbows were propped on his knees and he held a small blue towel in his hands.

Dear heaven, she thought, she was stunned by what Debbie and Jerome had just told her. The students that Joe was so dedicated to couldn't fathom why he was living where he was if he didn't have to. Joe felt it was the only way to really relate to these kids, make them trust and believe in him.

But she now knew that Joe had sentenced himself to a life-style of having far less than he was able to for no concrete purpose. The students at Lincoln certainly wouldn't think less of him for having a nice home uptown, as Jerome had put it.

In fact, they might even respect him more than they did if he showed them that working hard to become a teacher was a guaranteed ticket out of the dreary ghetto.

Oh, dear, dear, what should she do? Polly wondered frantically. Tell Joe what she'd learned while sitting in that noisy gym? Not "mess in his business," because she was definitely *not* his lady? She had to think this through, pro and con it, sift and sort.

A loud buzzer blasted and Polly jumped in surprise, the jarring sound bringing her from her troubled reverie.

"Halftime," Jerome said. "We're ahead by four points. That's not enough of a lead against those guys."

"Look at the bright side," Polly said. "It's better than being behind by four points."

Joe stood and began to follow his players to the locker room. He turned his head, sent a big smile in Polly's direction, then continued on his way.

"Mercy, mercy, mercy," Debbie said, dissolving in a fit of laughter. "Did you catch that, Jerome? Whoa. Knock yourself out, Coach. And here you are, Bird Lady, trying to tell us you're not Coach Dillon's lady. Come Monday morning, everybody at Lincoln is going to know that the coach has himself a woman. Isn't that fine?"

"It's a fact," Jerome said, getting to his feet. "I'm going outside."

"Don't get into anything with those uptown kids out there, Jerome," Debbie said. "You keep your mouth shut, you hear?"

"Yeah, yeah," Jerome said, moving away.

"Oh, that man gives me fits," Debbie said.

"You and Jerome are planning to get married?" Polly said.

"Oh, my, yes," Debbie said. "We're graduating from Lincoln in June, getting married and moving on."

"What are you going to do?" Polly said. "I mean, are you thinking about college?"

"No, we don't have money for that. Jerome can fix anything on wheels, so we figure he can get a good paying job as a mechanic. I was planning to be a waitress, or whatever, until we have a baby. But then, you know, well, you came to that career day thing at school and... Oh, forget it."

"No, go on," Polly said. "I'd like to think we're becoming friends, Debbie. Why don't you call me Polly, instead of Bird Lady? What were you going to say?"

"Well, you've got a career even though you didn't

have much money starting out. Tending to stupid birds would sure beat waiting tables."

Polly frowned. "You really believe that all I do is take care of pampered, expensive birds?"

Debbie shrugged. "That and clean up after a bunch of rich folks' pets. Hey, you do what you have to when you're short on money." She paused. "No, maybe I'll just wait tables. I can't stomach the idea of bowing and scraping to megabucks folks all day. I'll work in a café where my kind of people eat."

"You…you think I sold out, don't you?" Polly said quietly. "Joe…Coach Dillon said that you, the students at Lincoln, would feel that way about me."

"I'm not messing in your business, Polly. You gotta do what you gotta do. But me and Jerome? He'll be a hotshot mechanic and I'll be a waitress. And we're going to have the cutest baby that was ever born. We're not raising our kid in the ghetto, either. We're going to be fine, just fine. We might even have our own furniture someday. Nice stuff, really classy."

"I'm sure you will," Polly said. "Debbie, listen, I took the job at Dogwood Veterinary Clinic because it paid well, and I have a brother and sister counting on me for financial help to attend college."

"Oh. Well, that makes sense, I guess. Thing is, Polly, are you going to stop tending to dumb birds when your family doesn't need your money anymore?"

"I…"

"Know how I see it?" Debbie said, squinting into space. "Coach Dillon is living poor in the ghetto when he doesn't have to. You're going to stay elbow to elbow with folks that aren't your own long past when you need to be doing that. You and the coach are both operating where you don't belong. Sure is going to be tough for you two to get together and have yourself a cute little baby. That's a shame. It truly is.''

"But…"

The buzzer sounded again and the two teams filed back into the gym from the locker rooms.

Good grief, Polly thought, taking a steadying breath, *my brain is on overload.* Was Debbie a wise-beyond-her-years young woman, or just a nonsense-filled adolescent?

Had she, Polly Chapman, stepped into a world far removed from her roots with the subconscious knowledge that she never intended to leave?

Was she as guilty of going too far in the wrong direction as Joe Dillon was?

So many questions without answers.

Joe walked by and flashed Polly another smile, which earned her a poke in the ribs from a giggling Debbie.

And there was another question, Polly thought, watching Joe settle onto the bench. What was she going to do about the emotional and sensual spell that Joe was slowly, but surely, weaving around her?

Six

The third quarter of the basketball game began and the noise in the gymnasium was on high volume. The students from both schools realized that their teams had come to play, and play tough, and the tension and excitement mounted with every shot of the ball.

Polly could feel the vibration of the bleacher beneath her bottom as the fans pounded their feet on the wooden benches, while hollering at the top of their lungs. Each side was attempting to outdo the other, with pretty cheerleaders urging them on.

It was bedlam.

And Polly was having a wonderful time.

She chanted the cheers that she remembered from her own school days, and applauded during those that were new. She screamed at the referees for injustices she was convinced were being directed at the Abraham Lincoln Grizzlies, and spent more time on her feet than sitting down like the mature adult she'd promised Debbie and Jerome she'd be.

The score skittered back and forth. Lincoln ahead by six. Copper ahead by four. Lincoln gaining the lead by two, and on and on.

When the buzzer sounded, marking the end of the third quarter, Polly sank onto the bench and fanned her hand in front of her heated, flushed face.

The game was tied at seventy-two all.

"Polly," Debbie said.

"Whew! Playing basketball is exhausting, isn't it, Debbie?" Polly said happily. "I can't remember when I've had so much fun. Joe is an excellent coach, no doubt about it. He puts in exactly the right player for a given situation and…"

"Polly," Debbie said, tugging on her sleeve.

"Yes?" Polly said, looking at her. "Are you having a good time?"

"No. Jerome didn't come back after he went outside at halftime."

Polly glanced quickly at the empty space next to her on the bench, then stared wide-eyed at Debbie.

"I didn't even realize he wasn't there," Polly said. "I was so caught up in the game that—you're worried. I can tell from the expression on your face."

"You bet I am," Debbie said, fighting against threatening tears. "There's a big rivalry between Lincoln and Copper. We don't like them, they don't like us. I've got to go outside and find Jerome, make sure nothing has happened to him."

The buzzer shrilled and the fourth quarter of the game began.

"You can't go out there alone," Polly said, raising

her voice so Debbie could hear her. "I'll go with you. Come on."

The pair stood and made their way slowly along the bleacher, mumbling "Excuse me" as they wiggled past the exuberant fans. Finally making their way down to the floor, they hurried toward the bank of doors at the far end of the gym.

Joe stood and made a T out of his hands, indicating to his players to call a time-out. The referee caught the signal from the Grizzly player and blew his whistle, pointing to the Lincoln bench.

As Joe waited for his boys to hustle toward him, he indulged in another quick glance in Polly's direction, having thoroughly enjoyed observing her delightful and loud enthusiasm as she cheered on his team.

But Polly's seat was empty.

She was gone, and so were Debbie and Jerome.

Damn it, Joe thought, scanning the gym. Where was Polly? What in the hell was going on?

"Yeah, Coach?" one of the players said, breathing heavily.

"What?" Joe said. "Oh. Okay. Listen up. I thought that big center was finished for the night because of his bum knee. But they're obviously going to rotate him in and out. Whenever he comes in, double team him and leave that short guard open."

"Got it," the five boys said in unison.

"Go," Joe said, patting the nearest boy on the shoulder. "We can win this game. Stay tough. Stay focused. Don't foul."

Play resumed and Joe swept his gaze over the gymnasium once more before settling back onto the bench.

Ah, man, he thought, where in the hell was Polly?

*   *   *

The moment that Polly and Debbie stepped outside the gymnasium, Debbie grabbed Polly's hand, and Polly's heart began to race with fear.

Two police cars were parked at odd angles by the curb, blue lights whirling. A group of teenagers were being kept back in a controlled group by one of the officers, while three others were standing between the vehicles, blocking full view of two boys they were talking to.

Polly and Debbie moved forward cautiously, then Debbie gasped, as she tightened her hold on Polly's hand.

"Oh, God, Polly, look," she whispered, her voice trembling, "the cops have Jerome. He has blood on his shirt and…his face… Oh, his face is scraped and bleeding. He's been in a fight. They're going to take him to jail and never let him out." She burst into tears. "Oh, my poor Jerome. What are we going to do?"

"Stay calm," Polly said, her voice no steadier than Debbie's. She pried her fingers loose from Debbie's hand. "You wait right here and don't say one single word. Understand?"

Debbie sniffled and nodded. Polly shifted the strap of her purse higher on her shoulder, lifted her chin and marched toward the group standing between the cruisers.

"Good evening, Officers," she sang out, managing to produce a smile. "What seems to be the little problem here?" She slid a quick glare at Jerome, then glanced at the other boy, who was holding a bloody handkerchief to his nose. "Hmm?"

"We've got a couple of troublemakers on our hands," one of the policemen said. "We're taking them downtown. Who are you?"

"Ms. Polly Chapman. Now then, these young men are obviously juveniles, underage offenders, whom you will release to a person who is of authority in their lives. Correct? Yes, that is certainly the way it is."

Polly drew in a gulp of air.

"So!" she continued. "I'll just save everyone a lot of fuss and paperwork and take Jerome with me now. Come along, Jerome, you naughty boy. Just wait until I get you home, young man. Shame on you."

One of the officers raised a hand. "Hold it. I'm having a little problem believing that you're Jerome's mother, Ms. Chapman."

"You are?" she said, her eyebrows shooting up. "Oh, well, of course, you are. I'm not his mother. I'm his...his guardian. Yes!" Polly pointed one finger in the air. "That's who I am...Jerome's guardian."

A car came screeching up and the brakes were slammed on. A man barreled out of the driver's side.

"Oh-h-h, hell," the other boy said. "I'm dead meat. That's my dad."

The father stormed into the group. "One of your friends called me, Charles, and said you'd gotten into a fistfight with a kid from Lincoln. You idiot. I should let you spend the night in jail."

"I'm sorry, Dad," Charles said, keeping the soggy handkerchief pressed to his nose. His eyes filled with tears. "I don't want to go to jail, Dad. Please. Can't I just go home with you? I'm sorry. I'm really sorry. I swear I am."

"Officers?" Charles's father said, looking at each in turn.

"Well, we were going to take them in," one of the policemen said, "but...okay, take your son home." He looked at Polly. "And you, guardian of Jerome, get your kid out of here."

"I will, I will. Thank you," Polly said, smiling. "Thank you very much."

"As for you two," the officer addressed Jerome and Charles, "if there is any trouble from either of you in the future, you're going to find yourself in front of a juvenile court judge. Got that?"

Jerome and Charles nodded vigorously. Charles's father hustled the teenager toward the car.

"Come on, Jerome," Polly said. "We're going home. Right now."

"Ms. Chapman?" one of the policemen said.

"Yes, sir?"

"You're a lousy liar," he said, unable to curb his smile. "I don't recommend you make a habit of it."

"Oh," Polly said, in a small voice. "I won't. I mean, I don't. This was an emergency situation that called for desperate measures."

"Right," the officer said, chuckling. "Haul your felon away."

"We're gone," Polly said, grabbing Jerome's arm. "You'll never see, or hear, from us again. Bye."

Polly propelled Jerome to the sidewalk, where Debbie threw her arms around him in a hug, then a moment later stepped back and slugged him on the arm.

"Stop that," Polly whispered, "or we'll all end up in the clink. You can holler at him later, Debbie. How did you two get to this side of town?"

"On the booster bus," Debbie said.

"Okay. You're coming home with me." Polly rummaged in her purse for a pen and a small notebook. She scribbled a message on a piece of the paper and tore it out. "Do you see someone you know from Lincoln in the group gathered over there?"

"At least half of those kids are from Lincoln," Debbie said.

"Then give this note to someone with a cool head," Polly said. "Tell them to slip it to Coach Dillon without making a major production out of it."

Debbie nodded, took the paper and ran to the group, returning quickly.

"Hurry up," Polly said, "before those policemen change their minds."

The three trotted toward the parking lot, Polly convinced that she heard a rumbling of police officer laughter drifting through the air after them.

When there were fifteen seconds left to play in the game, the score was tied at eighty-nine. The noise level in the gymnasium had risen to such a level that Joe had to cup his hands around his mouth and bellow at full-volume to his team on the court.

A feminine hand whipped suddenly over his right shoulder to shove a small, folded piece of paper an inch in front of his nose. Joe grabbed the paper, turned quickly to receive a big smile from a pretty girl, then redirected his attention to the game.

"One shot," he yelled. "No fouls. One shot."

Five seconds remained on the clock.

Four…

Three…

"Now, Luis," Joe said, under his breath. "Set your feet. Shoot it. Now!"

The ball arched through the air, seemed to hang suspended for a heart-stopping moment, then swished through the basket without touching the rim.

The final buzzer blared.

The Abraham Lincoln Grizzlies had won the game.

"Yes!" Joe shouted.

He punched one fist in the air as he lunged to his feet. The students from Lincoln poured out of the bleachers to surround the five players on the court, the remaining team on the bench joining the celebration.

Joe stayed where he was, allowing the team to bask in their glory, while giving him the opportunity to read the mysterious note.

"What in the…" he said aloud, his eyes widening as he read the missive.

"Joe," the message said, "Jerome in a bit of trouble. Have taken him and Debbie to my apartment. Polly."

Joe frowned, bit back an expletive, then crumpled the paper in his fist. He made his way forward to start herding his team toward the locker room.

Polly smiled during the entire drive home as Debbie delivered a nonstop tirade at Jerome regarding his fist-fight with the Copper High School student. Wisely, Jerome simply nodded in total agreement and kept his mouth shut.

In Polly's living room, Debbie stopped statue still and looked around.

"Oh, Polly," she said. "Wow. Awesome. This apartment is yours, all yours? You don't have to share it with anyone?"

"It's mine," Polly said. "The furniture is used and the rooms aren't very big, but I really like it."

"Awesome," Debbie repeated. "Don't you think so, Jerome? We might have a place like this someday."

"It's cool," Jerome said. "Oh, my eye, my head. I'm

dying here. The other guy is worse off, though. Guaranteed.''

"Oh, shut up," Debbie said. "I don't want to hear one more word about that fight."

"Me, either," Jerome said. "You were the one going on about it all the way here, not me."

"Enough of that," Polly said. "Come into the kitchen so we can tend to your face, Jerome."

"What he deserves is a bite on the butt from that bird of yours, Polly," Debbie said.

Polly laughed and the trio headed for the kitchen.

Thirty minutes later, Jerome's face had been washed, a bandage put on a cut above a swelling right eye, and they were all consuming ham-and-cheese sandwiches along with cans of soda.

A brisk knock sounded at the door. Polly got to her feet and hurried to answer the already repeated summons. She flung open the door to find a deeply scowling Joe Dillon standing before her.

"Hi," she greeted him brightly.

"Mmm," Joe said, moving past her. "Jerome, you are on my list, buddy."

"Uh-oh," Debbie said.

Joe strode into the kitchen with Polly right on his heels.

"I'm sorry, Coach," Jerome said, getting to his feet. "I really am. The jerk from Copper started it—I swear he did. He was taunting me, was all over my case, really giving me a hard time. I ignored him until he said what he did about you."

"Me?" Joe said, surprise evident on his face.

"Well, yeah, see, he said that you hold that blue towel during the game to keep from…well, um, from sucking your thumb. When he said that, I busted his nose."

"Oh, dear, dear," Polly said, bursting into laughter. "Oops," she added, when Joe shot her a dark glare. "So sorry."

Joe sighed. "Okay. What's done, is done. Believe it or not, the booster bus followed me over here. You two haul it outside and get on that bus. *After* you thank Ms. Chapman for saving your tail, Jerome."

"Thank you, Polly," Debbie said, hugging her. "You're wonderful and we're really, truly friends now."

"Thank you, Polly," Jerome said. "I sure wasn't into going to jail." He looked at Joe. "You've picked yourself a fine woman, Coach. Your lady is something else. Special, you know what I mean? Very cool."

"Go!" Joe said, pointing to the door.

"Is the team bus out there, too?" Debbie said.

"No," Joe said. "I'm going to have enough explaining to do for rerouting the booster bus. I didn't know what to expect when I arrived here so...Mr. Franklin from school and his wife were at the game. Mrs. Franklin drove their car, and Mr. Franklin went back on the team bus. You've put a lot of people through a great deal of inconvenience, Jerome. I hope you realize that."

"I was protecting your honor, Coach!"

Joe was unable to keep from smiling. "Sucking my thumb, huh? What a stupid thing to say."

"Yeah, well, he has a busted nose to show for his big, stupid mouth," Jerome said.

"Okay, okay, go get on that bus."

With another flurry of goodbyes and thank-yous, Debbie and Jerome left the apartment. A sudden and heavy silence fell over the kitchen.

"So!" Polly said. "Did we win the game?"

"Yeah," Joe said, chuckling. "We won."

"Oh, that's super, just great. Would you like a ham-and-cheese sandwich?"

"Sure," Joe said. "Thank you."

"Sit down at the table and I'll fix it. It will be ready in a jiffy."

Joe settled onto one of the chairs and watched Polly as she prepared the food.

Did *we* win the game? his mind echoed. For some unexplainable reason, his heart had seemed to skip a beat when Polly had said *we* in regard to winning, or losing, the basketball game.

A strange warmth had suffused him at the same time. There was a sense of sharing and caring about the way Polly had said *we*. It had been *their* game, with him coaching the boys and Polly cheering them on.

It felt good, really good.

Ah, Dillon, knock it off, Joe told himself, dragging both hands down his face. He was coming down from an emotional high, that's all. He was always wired after coaching a game until he could get home, alone, to relax and unwind.

But tonight?

He wasn't alone. He was in Polly Chapman's kitchen about to consume a ham-and-cheese sandwich.

And this, too, felt very, very good.

Dillon, that is definitely enough nonsense, he thought. *Quit thinking. Eat the dumb sandwich, then get the hell out of here and go home where you belong.*

Home? his mind echoed suddenly. That dreary little place in that gray, dreary neighborhood? Yeah, that was what he called home, all right, in all its shabby glory.

He'd fixed it up as best he could, but there was just so much anyone could do with a place like that. The pipes were rusting out, the wiring was shot—blew a fuse

if he turned on more than two lights at the same time—
and a new crack in the kitchen ceiling had appeared just
last week.

That was home?

Joe glanced around Polly's apartment.

There was a warmth here, he mused, despite its small
size and threadbare furniture. It welcomed a person, sort
of wrapped itself around him with an undefinable something that made him want to linger, soak it up, allow it
to soothe.

His home sure as hell didn't do that for him. In fact,
it *wasn't* a home, it was a house, and a crummy one, at
that.

Lord, Dillon, he admonished himself, where was all
this coming from? It was as though, after all these years,
he was taking a long, hard look at where he lived and
had found it sadly lacking.

Damn it, why was he doing this to himself? Did it
have something to do with the emergence of Polly Chapman into his life? Hell, he didn't know. That woman
was definitely muddling his brain.

"There you are," Polly said, bringing Joe from his
tangled, troubled thoughts.

She set a plate, a can of soda and a glass in front of
Joe, then sat down opposite him.

"I hope you won't stay angry at Jerome," she said.
"Look at the bright side. You didn't have to bail him
out of jail."

"Thanks to you." Joe took a bite of the sandwich,
chewed and swallowed. "Your stepping in the way you
did was a very decent thing to do, Polly. I appreciate it.
One of the students told me they heard you tell the cops
that you were Jerome's guardian."

Polly laughed. "They wouldn't believe that I was his

mother. Actually, they didn't buy my story of being his guardian, either, but they decided to allow me to... quote...haul my felon away.''

''Why did you do it? You don't even know Debbie and Jerome.''

''Oh, but I do.'' Polly leaned slightly toward Joe. ''When I arrived at the gym, they stood up and waved, then gestured to me to come sit with them. I was so touched, so... Well, it meant a great deal to me.''

Joe nodded, looking at Polly intently as he continued to eat.

''I deal with animals all day,'' Polly continued, ''that belong to other people. A dog might lick my hand, a cat purr and lean against me, but Debbie and Jerome are people, real people. They extended their friendship to me with no reservations. When Jerome got into trouble, helping him was as natural as breathing.''

Joe drained the soda can, then set it on the table, staring at it for a long moment before meeting Polly's gaze again.

''I think,'' he said quietly, ''that you're beginning to understand why the kids at Lincoln mean so much to me, are so important.''

''Yes,'' Polly said softly, ''I think maybe I am.''

Joe got to his feet and moved around the table to draw Polly up and into his arms. She went willingly, and when his mouth claimed hers, she returned his kiss eagerly.

Oh, dear, dear, how heavenly, Polly thought dreamily, as heated desire thrummed instantly throughout her. Hello, Joe. *I've missed you, Joe.*

Joe raised his head a fraction of an inch to speak close to Polly's lips, his voice gritty with passion.

''You're my hummingbird,'' he said. ''You're so delicate, so fragile, yet so strong and determined when you need to be.''

He captured her lips once again in a searing kiss.

A hummingbird for Joe, Polly thought. How lovely, how beautiful that sounded.

Then all rational thought fled.

Hearts beat with wild tempos and their breathing became labored, echoing in the small, quiet room. The embers of desire from the previous night were fanned into licking flames that burned even hotter than the night before. They were on fire, consumed with passion that was demanding to be satisfied.

Joe broke the kiss to draw a ragged breath.

''I want you, Polly,'' he said. ''I want to make love with you.''

''Yes. Yes, I want you, too.''

''Are you certain that you…''

''Shh. Yes.''

He lifted her into his arms as easily as though she weighed no more than the hummingbird he'd spoken of. He carried her into the bedroom, set her on her feet, then swept back the blankets on the bed. The light from the lamp in the living room cast a golden glow over them and the bed.

They shed their clothes quickly, then stilled, standing a foot apart, drinking in the sight of each other.

''Ah, Polly,'' Joe said finally, extending his hand toward her.

She placed her hand in his and smiled at him warmly, trustingly.

He lifted her into his arms again and placed her in the center of the bed, following her down to seek and find her lips. He rested his weight on one forearm, his other hand splayed on Polly's flat stomach.

So soft, Joe thought. Polly was femininity personified. She was, indeed, as tiny and fragile as a hummingbird. He would be so gentle with her, so careful not to hurt her with his rough-edged, muscled body.

Polly, sweet, sweet Polly.

Polly trailed her fingertips over Joe's back, marveling at the feel of the taut skin and bunching muscles.

What a glorious man, she thought. He was perfectly proportioned with wide shoulders, well-defined biceps, narrow hips and powerful legs. He was the epitome of man.

And she was going to make wondrous love with Joe Dillon.

It was right, so very right.

Desires soared as kisses intensified. Hands roamed, caressing and discovering. It was ecstasy.

Joe shifted to one of Polly's small, firm breasts, laving the nipple with his tongue. She closed her eyes, savoring the heated sensations sweeping throughout her. She sank her fingertips into Joe's thick hair, pressing his mouth harder onto her soft, sensitive flesh.

''Oh, my,'' she whispered.

He moved to her other breast, as his hand skimmed along her slender hip, then across her stomach. His fingers inched lower, finding her moist heat. His muscles ached from the self-restraint he was executing and he ignored the pain…wanting, needing to know, that Polly was ready to receive him.

Her pleasure would come first, Joe mentally vowed, because this was Polly and she deserved to be treated reverently, gently, with the awe and wonder due her.

''Oh, Joe, please,'' Polly whispered, clutching his shoulders.

"Yes," Joe said, raising his head, "I'm going up in flames. I want you so damn much."

"And I want you, too, so very much. Come to me, Joe."

He entered her slowly, his muscles trembling. Polly raised her hips to meet him. And Joe was lost. He surged into her and began to move in a thundering tempo, Polly meeting him beat for beat.

It was as old as time, and it was new and theirs alone. It was perfection, so intimate, pure and simplistic, yet so complex as emotions tumbled through the maze of sensuousness.

It was Polly and Joe, one entity.

They soared higher, reaching for the summit, then bursting upon it seconds apart, clinging to each other, holding fast.

"Joe!"

"Ah, Polly."

They lingered, hovered, drifted, then floated back slowly to now.

Joe kissed Polly gently, reverently, then moved off her, settling her close to his side. She sighed in sated contentment.

"Oh, Joe," she said, awe evident in her voice.

"I know," he said, sifting his fingers through her hair.

"Sleepy."

"Then sleep, little hummingbird," he whispered, kissing her on the forehead.

Within moments, Polly's even breathing told Joe that she had drifted off into blissful slumber. He frowned as he felt the turmoil in his weary mind gaining force, hammering at him.

Ah, man, he thought, he was such a mental mess. He was suddenly dissatisfied, judgmental, about his meager dwelling by Lincoln high. Did the fact that he couldn't stand up to his full height in his lousy shower make him a better teacher?

Ah, hell, why was he questioning his life-style now? Why now?

And if that wasn't enough to send him over the edge of his sanity, there was Polly and the exquisitely beautiful lovemaking they'd just shared. Lovemaking that had been entwined with foreign and unfamiliar emotions that were so powerful they had caused an ache to close his throat.

Dear Lord, what was happening to him? He felt like a stranger in his own body. He was smothering under the weight of the turmoil of confusion in his mind.

He had to get out of there, be alone, attempt to somehow, *somehow,* create some order in his thinking before he was beyond thinking clearly at all.

Moving carefully so as not to awaken Polly, Joe left the bed and dressed quickly. He stood for a moment, staring at the lovely woman who had given of herself so freely, openly and honestly.

Then he spun on his heel and strode from the room.

Seven

Polly stirred and opened her eyes, blinking several times to bring herself fully awake.

Joe, she thought, as the last foggy cobwebs of sleep dissolved.

She turned her head on the pillow, frowned when she saw the empty expanse of bed next to her, then smiled in the next instant.

Maybe Joe had something on his calendar this morning, she thought. He had no doubt left a note for her somewhere in the apartment that would explain his without-a-word-spoken-to-her exit.

Polly stretched like a lazy kitten, mentally reliving the exquisite lovemaking shared with Joe. How glorious it had been. They had come together like two perfectly synchronized dancers, moving as one, meshed, soaring to wondrous heights of ecstasy.

"Oh-h-h, my," Polly said dreamily.

Still smiling, she left the bed and headed for the bathroom. After showering and dressing in jeans and a pale pink sweater, she went in search of Joe's note and a hot cup of coffee.

Fifteen minutes later Polly sat at the kitchen table, a mug of coffee cradled in her hands as she propped her elbows on the table. Her smile had long since disappeared, having been replaced by a frown and a chill that had gripped her heart with a painful fist.

She had searched everywhere…twice…for a note from Joe. But she hadn't found one, because he hadn't written one. He'd simply left her, her bed and home, and disappeared into the night.

Oh, dear heaven, Polly thought miserably. It couldn't be true, could it? Surely not. No. But the evidence was before her in stark reality. She, Polly Chapman, had been a one-night stand for Joe Dillon.

With trembling hands, Polly set the mug on the table with exacting care so as not to spill the hot liquid.

She pressed her fingertips to her lips, willing herself not to cry, not to react like the unsophisticated woman she knew herself to be.

Look at the bright side, she told herself frantically. She would do that, just as soon as she could figure out what the elusive bright side was.

Darn it, darn it, darn it, she had no one to blame for this but herself. She'd known from the onset that Joe was out of her league. He knew women like Celine, who executed air-kisses with expertise and called Joe ''darling,'' while babbling on about skiing trips to Aspen.

Making love—having sex to be more precise—was probably no big deal to Joe. He was accustomed to women fawning over him and hopping into his bed with no-strings-attached enthusiasm.

Polly sniffled, plunked one elbow back onto the table and rested her chin in the palm of her hand.

She'd had no intention of attempting to attach any strings to Joe. Mercy, no. She knew, somewhere in her muddled mind, that they had no real future together, nothing permanent, no fairy-tale forever and ever.

But for Joe to leave her bed, then walk out her door without a word, a note, a something? Oh, that was so rotten, so tacky. She was humiliated, mortified, embarrassed…and mad as hell.

Polly lifted her chin from the cradle of her palm, then smacked the table with her hand, causing the coffee to slosh over the edge of the mug.

"Drat," she said, getting to her feet.

She crossed the kitchen to snatch a paper towel from the holder mounted beneath one of the cabinets, then stomped back to wipe up the spilled coffee.

"I'm mad, not sad," she said, as she cleaned up the mess she'd made. "Therefore, I won't cry, because tears are for sad, and I'm mad, not sad. But…" she sniffled again "…if this is a contest between mad and sad, I think sad is winning."

A knock sounded at the door and Polly glared in the direction of the noise.

Whoever it was, she decided, she was in no mood for chitchat. She'd just pretend she wasn't home and they'd go away.

The knock was repeated.

Oh, dear, dear, she thought, maybe it was her sister, or brother, or someone who might wonder and worry about her absence so early on a Sunday morning.

With a sigh of defeat, she dropped the soggy paper towel onto the table and went to open the door.

Joe shifted the sack he was holding from one arm to the other in a restless, edgy gesture.

He glanced heavenward, sending a silent plea that his insistent knocking was waking Polly from a deep, contented slumber. If that could be true, then she'd not yet know that he wasn't next to her in the bed.

He'd driven home last night, showered, then gone to bed, fully expecting to fall asleep quickly. Instead, he'd tossed and turned, then ended up calling himself every low-life name in the book.

As early as was conceivably reasonable, he'd gone to the store, then returned to Polly's, driving above the speed limit.

He was such scum, he thought. At some point in the seemingly endless night, he'd reached the conclusion that he shouldn't see Polly again, due to the inner turmoil that raged within him by being with her.

And another thing had become crystal clear during the sleepless hours. Polly was a hearth-home-and-babies woman, and he could never offer her that world, no matter where their emotions might take them. He had chosen his life-style and it would remain as it was.

Wouldn't it?

Yes, damn it, it would.

He had nothing to offer Polly Chapman.

Then later, as he continued to stare into the darkness, he realized that his hasty exit from Polly's, without a word or a note, gave every indication that he considered their lovemaking a one-night stand. What a sleaze.

Polly was entitled to, and would have, an explanation as to why it was impossible for them to see each other again. That conversation would go much more smoothly if his pounding on the door was just now waking Polly up.

The apartment door was opened.

Damn, Joe thought, as he saw a fully-dressed Polly Chapman standing before him.

"Hi," he said, forcing a lightness to his voice and a smile onto his face. "Ready for some breakfast?"

Polly opened her mouth, closed it, then tried again.

"Pardon me?" she said.

Joe stepped into the living room and headed for the kitchen. Polly shut the door, then followed him, definitely frowning.

"Joe, what…?"

"I went home, showered and put on fresh clothes," he said, setting the sack on the counter. Which was true. He'd simply refrain from mentioning what time he'd actually left Polly's apartment. "I have a gourmet breakfast for us here, sweet Polly. Strawberries, bagels and cream cheese. How's that?"

He turned to see Polly standing stiff as a pencil by the table, her hands wrapped around her elbows in a closed, protective manner.

Ah, look at her, Joe thought, his heart thundering. There was his precious, fragile hummingbird. He wanted to cross the room, pull her into his arms and kiss her senseless.

He'd tell her how sensational their lovemaking had been and would sincerely mean every word. He'd kiss away that stricken, confused expression on her face until it was replaced by one of Polly's sunshine smiles.

Easy, Dillon, he told himself. *Get a grip.* That eerie, sensuous spell that Polly was capable of weaving around him was beginning to cloud his mind, cause him to for-

get why he was there, what he had to say. To continue
to date Polly wasn't fair to her, served no purpose in the
overall picture of the future.

But, ah, damn it, this was going to be tough. The
thought of never seeing Polly again was suddenly causing a knot to twist painfully in his gut.

To never make love with Polly again? Never hear her
lilting laughter? Watch her blue eyes dance with merri-
ment, then become smoky gray with desire?

Walking away from Polly was asinine, really stupid
and totally unacceptable.

No, wait a minute. That was selfishness on his part.
He knew he couldn't offer Polly what she deserved to
have. He knew that. He had to end this now, this morning.

Well, there was no sense in wasting the food he'd
bought, Joe reasoned. Conversations like the one on his
agenda were better conducted on a full stomach. They'd
eat, then talk. Fine.

"Polly?" Joe said. "Do you like strawberries? Bagels?"

"What? Oh, yes, sure I do."

Joe crossed the room to grip Polly gently by the shoulders.

"You're upset, aren't you?" he said quietly. "Are
you regretting that we made love? Tell me what you're
thinking, what's on your mind."

"I'm not sorry we made love," Polly said, meeting
Joe's gaze. "It was beautiful, very special. It's just that
when I woke up this morning and you were gone, and
there wasn't even a note from you, I felt—well, I thought
what we'd shared had been nothing more than just a one-
night stand to you."

"Ah, sweet Polly, no." Joe wrapped his arms around

her and drew her close. Polly encircled his waist with her arms and rested her head on his chest. "I didn't take our lovemaking lightly, believe me. It was very beautiful and special for me, too."

Polly tilted her head back to look up at him.

"Really?" she said.

Joe lowered his lips toward hers.

"Really," he said, then covered her mouth with his.

The kiss was an explosion of heated passion. It instantly fanned glowing embers of desire still lingering from the night before into hot, licking flames that consumed them.

Joe broke the kiss and eased Polly away from his aroused body.

"We have to talk," he said, his voice gritty. "Sit down at the table and I'll spread out our breakfast."

Polly did as instructed and Joe opened cupboards and drawers to find a bowl, plates and knives. The enticing meal was soon on the table between them, and their mugs were filled with coffee.

"Dig in," Joe said.

"What do we have to talk about?" Polly said.

"Let's eat first."

"Why?"

Joe frowned. "You're not cooperating, Polly. Have a strawberry."

"How can I eat when you've said 'we have to talk' in such an ominous tone of voice?"

"It wasn't ominous. It was serious, befitting the subject matter."

"Which is…?" Polly said, leaning slightly toward him and raising her eyebrows.

"We can't see each other anymore," Joe blurted out. "Oh, hell, nice going, Dillon."

Polly sank back in her chair, her eyes widening.

"You show up here," she said, "with a romantic breakfast of strawberries and bagels, tell me that our lovemaking was as beautiful and special for you as it was for me, then announce that we can't see each other anymore? Does that make sense? No, it certainly does not."

Joe captured one of Polly's hands with his on the top of the table.

"Yes, it does, Polly. Listen to me, okay? Hear me out. You've become very important to me very quickly, and that's not good. It's bad, very bad. What if we fall in love with each other? Did it ever occur to you what a disaster that would be?"

"It would?" she said, frowning. "Why?"

"Polly, come on. You've seen where I live. You know what my focus, what my purpose is. There's no room in my life for love...for falling in love, marrying, having a wife and family. You deserve a husband, home, babies. I can't give you any of those things."

"But..."

"Our being together is dangerous, don't you understand? What if our emotions run away with our sense of reason? It would be a mess, a heartbreaking experience."

"Oh." Polly paused. "Joe, there's something I think you ought to know."

"What is it?"

"At the basketball game last night, Debbie and Jerome told me that none of the kids at Lincoln can understand why you live in the ghetto when you don't have to. They like and respect you very much, but just can't get a handle on why you stay in that neighborhood."

"You're kidding," Joe said, feeling as though he'd been punched in the gut.

"No, I'm not. I'm sorry. I know you thought you could relate better to those students by living down there but...I'm sorry, Joe. It doesn't have anything to do with us not seeing each other again, I guess, but I thought you had the right to know what Debbie and Jerome said to me."

Joe got to his feet and began to pace around the small kitchen. He dragged a restless hand through his hair, then shook his head.

"I don't believe this," he said, not halting his trek. "Why didn't any of them approach me, say something to me about it?"

"Because they 'don't mess in anyone's business,'" Polly said, watching him intently. "That's a direct quote. They think the world of you, Joe—I could tell that they do. You should feel very proud, very fulfilled, regarding the impact you've had on the lives of so many young people all these years."

"All these years," he repeated, with a bark of laughter that echoed his self-disgust. "There I was...oh, yeah, living the life, walking the walk, talking the talk. Lord, what a patronizing, condescending, supercilious jerk I've been."

"Joe, don't be so hard on yourself. Your heart and mind were in the right place. You were just too close to see it clearly, view it all through the eyes of those kids. I have to admit that I wondered why you insisted on living down there, too. You're continually urging them to stay in school, work hard, provide themselves with a ticket out of that neighborhood, that life-style.

"They know you make a decent wage as a teacher. They understandably can't fathom why you live there when you don't have to, especially since you encourage them to do everything within their power to be able to leave. They don't think less of you. They're confused by it, that's all.''

Joe spun around and looked at Polly, planting his hands on his hips.

"You must be loving this," he said, a rough edge to his voice. "I was on your case about selling out, taking a job where pets are pampered like rich babies. I also got in a dig or two regarding the fact that you've settled for being less than you could be in your chosen profession. You must be having a hard time keeping from laughing right out loud as I'm getting my comeuppance in spades.''

Polly frowned. "I'm finding no pleasure in witnessing your distress, Joe.''

"No? Well, how about dishing out one of your famous 'look at the bright side' deals, Pollyanna?''

Polly got to her feet. "That's enough. You're upset and you're taking it out on me in a kill-the-messenger syndrome. What would you have had me do, Joe? Keep silent about what Debbie and Jerome told me?''

"Yes!" he said, nearly yelling. He shook his head and lowered the volume of his voice. "No. No, of course, not. Hell, I don't know. I need some time alone to think this through. I'm going to leave now, but I'll talk to you later.''

"Oh?" Polly said, folding her arms beneath her breasts. "Is that so? What happened to your declaration that we can't see each other anymore?''

"Polly, I'm so damn confused right now that I'm not in a mental position to make a sensible, rational statement about anything.''

Joe closed the distance between them, gripped Polly's

shoulders and nearly lifted her off her feet as he kissed her deeply. When he finally released her, Polly almost toppled over.

"Later," Joe said gruffly. "I'll call you."

He strode from the room, and moments later Polly heard the front door close with a bang.

"Gracious," she said, sinking onto her chair.

She placed one hand on her heart, waiting for it to return to a normal tempo after going into overdrive from Joe's departing kiss. That accomplished, she took a bite of a big, juicy strawberry and stared into space.

"Oh, dear, dear," she said aloud, "everything is suddenly so complicated."

She sighed and reached for another strawberry.

Joe wasn't the only one who had some serious thinking to do, she realized. She needed to get in touch with herself to discover the depth of her growing feelings for Joe—*dangerous* growing feelings.

There was also the matter of what had happened the previous night with Debbie and Jerome. She had been so...so touched by the fact that she'd been able to step in and help those young people.

She could still feel the warmth that had suffused her when Debbie had expressed her gratitude by giving Polly a heartfelt hug. "You're wonderful,' Debbie had said, "and we're really, truly friends now."

Polly sighed as her fingers grasped another strawberry.

It had been a very long time, she mused, since she'd reached out to another human being. She'd been devoting herself to animals and silly birds like Jazzy. They were safe, those pampered pets, didn't belong to her, couldn't disappoint her, wouldn't ask more of her than she was capable of giving.

All her life, it seemed, she'd had to reach deeply

within herself to find the ever famous bright side to make things all right.

When she was anticipating her eighth birthday, she'd stopped every day on the way home from school to stand next to a candy-apple red bicycle on display in a store in the neighborhood.

Oh, how she'd wanted that bike. She'd envisioned herself whizzing along the sidewalk, her braids flying in the wind, as everyone watched Polly Chapman on her marvelous red bike.

Her birthday had come and there was, indeed, a bike from her parents. But it was pea-soup green, a used one they had scrubbed up, adding a pretty white wicker basket on the front.

With tears of disappointment aching in her throat, she'd produced a beaming smile for her mother and father and thanked them profusely. They had done the best they could do, she knew that. There just wasn't enough money for shiny, new candy-apple red bicycles.

Through the years there had been clothes from resale shops instead of new outfits for school. She was always self-conscious as she wore what had been the fad in fashion the year before.

She'd listened with envy as her friends related exciting tales of vacation trips during the summer. The Chapman family had gone to the drive-in movies, taking popcorn made in their kitchen at home.

Even her dream of being a veterinarian had fallen just short of total fulfillment as she settled for the degree of Veterinary Technician.

It was no one's fault, Polly thought, pulling the dish of strawberries closer. Her parents had done the very best they could under their circumstances.

But she'd grown so tired, so inwardly weary, of continually having to set things to rights, make them acceptable in her mind. She'd become a pro at being Pollyanna Polly. She knew how to protect herself from the pain of disappointment.

She'd even carried her shield into the social arena. She dated men who were not in a position to promise her anything. No promises made meant no dreams to hold fast to, only to have them sift away like sand falling into oblivion through fingers unable to grasp tightly enough to keep it forever.

So she'd lavished her loving emotions on animals, knowing they'd not ask her to believe in them for more than the moment at hand.

But now? Polly thought, nibbling on yet another strawberry. Now there was Joe.

They had laughed together, squabbled together, and shared lovemaking together that had been more exquisitely beautiful than anything she'd experienced before.

Now there was Joe.

He could set her on fire with a look. Dissolve her bones with a kiss. He'd introduced her to the world he existed in, and made her feel young, excited and vibrantly alive as she'd cheered on the basketball team from Abraham Lincoln High School. He'd given her Debbie and Jerome, who had captured her heart with a hug.

Now there was Joe.

She deserved a husband, home and babies, he had said. As those words had tiptoed through her heart, mind and soul, she'd forgotten to keep her protective wall in place. In her vulnerable, exposed state she'd known how deeply she wanted a family, wanted to love and be loved in return.

Joe was right, Polly thought miserably. They

shouldn't see each other anymore, because Joe Dillon was, inch by emotional inch, causing her to start to dream. To listen to her heart, instead of her head in regard to him. To see herself possibly having more, so much more, than she now had in her narrow existence.

What if we fall in love with each other? Did it ever occur to you what a disaster that would be?

Joe's words echoed in Polly's head and she nodded as she blinked away sudden, unwelcomed tears.

"Oh, yes," she whispered, "I understand now what a disaster that would be, Joe. There was no candy-apple red bicycle. I just can't believe there will be a forever-and-ever love for me, either."

Polly sniffled, then dipped her hand into the bowl of strawberries. Looking down, her eyes widened.

Oh, dear, dear, she thought, she'd just eaten an entire pint of strawberries, and her tummy was beginning to object to the overindulgence.

This was definitely *not* a day that had a bright side anywhere to be found.

Eight

Joe drove with no particular destination, finally weaving his way up the curving road in the Catalina Mountains that led to Mount Lemmon at the top.

He parked the car, then wandered aimlessly through the multitude of tall trees that boasted leaves of vibrant fall colors.

The mountain was at a high enough altitude to have the four seasons, including skiing in the winter. He made it a point to drive up there every November to enjoy the autumn foliage, but nature's beauty was lost on him this trip as he turned his thoughts inward, oblivious to the gorgeous scenery surrounding him.

Finally sitting on a boulder, Joe stared into space, then sighed.

Lord, he was tired, he thought. The fact that he'd hardly slept the night before, however, wasn't enough to make him feel so drained, so thoroughly exhausted.

His bone deep fatigue, he knew, stemmed from his inner turmoil. There were two enormous issues hammering away at his beleaguered brain.

One was Polly. Sweet Pollyanna Polly.

He'd returned to her apartment that morning to calmly explain why they should no longer see each other. He had, in fact, told her exactly that.

Then? he thought, shaking his head. He'd announced that he'd call her later, before he'd walked out the door. He'd said it. He'd meant it. He simply wasn't yet prepared to erase Polly Chapman from his life.

Why?

Hell, he didn't know.

Maybe it was connected to the second issue eating at him. The fact that he'd been living in the dinky little house near Abraham Lincoln High School for all these years for no justifiable reason.

His scaled-down life-style had accomplished nothing more than to cause the students he'd been attempting to relate to to shake their heads in confusion.

The kids respected and liked him, but considered him certifiably insane for staying in the ghetto when he possessed a paycheck that was his ticket out of that neighborhood.

Joe dragged his hands down his face, sighed again, then frowned.

How strange it was that he'd begun to question himself about living in that crummy house at the exact same time he'd learned the truth about the students' reaction to his oh-so-dedicated sacrifice.

Well, it was obviously time to move to a nice house in another section of town. So be it.

Which brought him full circle back to problem one...Polly.

His rationale for their not continuing their affair, relationship, whatever it was, was shot to hell. He'd informed her that she was aware of his focus, purpose, his dedication to the kids at Lincoln, as evidenced by his choice of living accommodations.

He could not, therefore, he had told her, offer her the husband, home and babies scenario that she most certainly deserved to have.

Now?

He was going to purchase a decent house in a safe, middle-class neighborhood. Said house would have trees, grass, a yard. Maybe he'd even get a dog.

That left a husband and babies missing from what he'd declared he was in no position to offer Polly.

Did he want to be a husband? Did he want to be a father? Was he falling in love with Polly, envisioning her, somewhere in the muddled mess of his mind, as his wife, his partner in life? How did Polly really, truly feel about him?

He just didn't know.

He'd been blindsided by Polly's disclosure of what Debbie and Jerome had said. That information in itself was enough to attempt to come to grips with. To discover that a firm stand he'd taken for nearly ten years had been so off base was very difficult to deal with, to say the least. And it was topped off by his own self-doubts about that decade-long decision.

He felt empty, hollow, Joe thought, as though an entire section of his being had been scooped out and tossed away as useless and unnecessary. He'd argued with his parents for years about where he chose to live for no discernable purpose.

No, he had no intention of reentering the jet-set fold occupied by Celine, Buffy, Ricky and the others. And, no, he wouldn't return to college to become an attorney, a clone of his father. He would continue to teach at Lincoln, where he knew he still belonged.

But beyond where he spent his days?

He'd be middle-class Joe Dillon, living in a middle-class house, in a middle-class neighborhood, mowing his middle-class lawn, and throwing a ball to his middle-class dog.

Did he want Polly in that middle-class picture? Would she even consider being there?

"Questions, questions, questions," Joe said aloud. He slid off the huge boulder. "And it's time to start getting some answers."

Polly sat on the sofa as Joe paced back and forth across her minuscule living room.

It was like watching a Ping-Pong game, she thought. Her living room wasn't big enough to compare this to a tennis match. Whatever the case, she was getting dizzy from keeping track of Joe's trek.

He'd telephoned her, stated briskly that they needed to talk, then arrived at her door twenty minutes later. He'd greeted her with a mumbled "hello" and a rather absentminded quick kiss, then began his endless pacing, not having spoken further.

"Excuse me," Polly said, "but I'm getting seasick from watching you wear out my already worn-out carpet, Joe. Do you think you could sit down. Please?"

"What?" Joe said, stopping where he was.

"Sit? Down? In a chair?"

"Oh. Yeah. Sure."

Joe settled onto the easy chair, crossed one ankle over his other knee, then dropped his foot back to the floor in the next instant. He leaned forward, propping his elbows on his knees and linking his fingers.

"I'm sitting," he said.

"Thank you."

"Polly," he said, "I want to apologize again for the distress I caused you this morning by leaving here without a word, then showing up again toting breakfast. Knowing that I upset you, combined with what you told me, has resulted in this being a very difficult day for me."

"I know," she said, sighing. "I feel very badly about that. I was the one to deliver the information from Debbie and Jerome. I'm so sorry, Joe."

"No, no, you did the right thing," he said. "I can't erase the past ten years, but at least I won't keep on making the same mistake for ten or twenty more."

"Well," Polly said, smiling, "that's a very healthy attitude."

"Which brings us to the subject of us, you and me."

Polly's smile disappeared.

"I know I said that we shouldn't see each other again," Joe continued, "but that was before I realized I was going far beyond what is necessary regarding my dedication to the kids at Lincoln. I have you to thank for waking me up about that."

"Oh, well, I was just passing along data I had, that's all."

"And I sincerely thank you for doing it." Joe paused. "Polly, my life is about to undergo major changes. I'll start shopping for a nice house in a good neighborhood right away, buy some decent furniture, the whole nine yards." He smiled. "I'm even going to get a dog."

Polly matched Joe's smile. "Really? A puppy? Oh,

how cute, how fun. What kind are you planning to get? What are you going to name it?''

"I don't know. The dog isn't the subject matter here. *We* are.''

Polly's smiled disappeared again.

"Something is happening between us," Joe said, looking directly at Polly. "It's very different from anything I've experienced before, and I want to know what it is. I think we should continue to see each other and discover exactly what we might, or might not, have together."

"Oh, dear, dear," Polly said. "Joe, you were the one who said that if we fell in love with each other it would be a disaster. Remember?"

"That was before you told me what Debbie and Jerome had said to you, added to doubts I was suddenly having myself. My entire existence—life-style—is going to change now."

"*Your's* is," Polly said, her voice rising, "but *mine* isn't."

Joe frowned. "What do you mean?"

"Did you ever wonder why I live in such a little apartment with threadbare furniture?"

"Yes, as a matter of fact, I did. I assumed you're well paid by the Dogwoods and could afford a better place than this one."

"Right," Polly said, nodding. "I could, but I can't."

"What?"

"Joe, I told you that I have a brother and sister, twins, who are freshmen at the U of A. They count on me for financial help to enable them to get an education. My parents are doing all they can, but Ted and Megan need the money I give them in order to make ends meet."

"I see," Joe said slowly.

Polly got to her feet and began to pace in the same circle that Joe had used during his trek around the small living room.

"Do you?" Polly said. "Do you really see? Do you really understand? I took the job with the highest salary offered to me. The heck with the fact that I tend to dumb birds and poodles with gourmet meals delivered by fancy restaurants. I make enough to have my own apartment *and* still be able to help out Ted and Megan."

"Polly…"

"Hush. I have the floor."

"You're wearing it out, just like I did," Joe said. "Why don't you sit back down so we can discuss this calmly?"

"No. There's nothing to calmly discuss. My sister and brother are just beginning college. There are years to go before they graduate, and I know exactly what I have to do during that time."

"But…"

"Quiet. I've always known what I've had to do, Joe. I'm not feeling sorry for myself, believe me. I've just learned to be realistic.

"There was no candy-apple red bicycle when I was eight years old, no new clothes while going to school. I've mastered how to make it all right, look at the bright side, be Pollyanna Polly.

"I can't, I mustn't, discover what you and I might mean to each other, because it isn't mine to have. Hopes and dreams, Joe, aren't part of my life. I have obligations, responsibilities that aren't going to go away."

Polly stopped and looked at Joe, swallowing past the sudden ache of tears in her throat.

"You were right in the first place," she said. "If we fell in love it would be a disaster, a heartbreaking experience. I...I can't see you anymore, Joe. It would be terribly foolish on my part.''

Joe got to his feet. Polly took a step backward and wrapped her hands around her elbows.

"No, don't," she said, her voice trembling. "Don't come over here, hold me, kiss me, make me incapable of thinking clearly. I know I'm doing the right thing by asking you to leave me alone.

"You have a whole new and exciting future before you now, and I hope you'll be very happy. My life has to go on exactly the way it is. There isn't room in my existence for love, for dreams of forever and ever. There just isn't, Joe.''

"Polly, you're wrong, dead wrong," Joe said, none too quietly. "Suppose, just suppose, we *did* fall in love, got married, planned to have a slew of babies to play with the dog. If that actually happened, then your family becomes mine.

"Don't you get it? I have money far beyond my wage as a teacher. I could put Ted and Megan through college with no problem.''

"Don't be ridiculous," Polly snapped. "I would never allow you to do that. That's absurd.''

"It is not!''

"Oh? And at what point would you wonder if I married you for your money?''

"Would you?" Joe said, his voice low. "Marry me for my money?''

"Of course not, you dolt. What a crummy question to ask." Polly executed an indignant little sniff. "That's extremely insulting.''

"You said it first," Joe said, with a burst of laughter. "It would never have occurred to me, because that's not who you are.''

"This is not a funny conversation, Mr. Dillon," Polly said, planting her hands on her hips. "This is a goodbye conversation, in case you've forgotten." She sniffled. "And there is nothing...nothing humorous about that."

Joe's smile changed to a frown. Despite Polly's directive not to come near her, he closed the distance between them and cradled her face in his hands.

Polly dropped her hands from her hips, but kept her arms at her sides, resisting the oh-so compelling urge to embrace Joe, savor the feel of him, the power and strength, his special, enticing aroma.

Joe looked directly into her eyes, and she was unable to tear her gaze from his.

"Polly," Joe said quietly, "so much is happening so quickly, changing, too, even in the short time we've known each other. I listened to what you said, really heard you. I know that you sincerely believe that the manner in which your life is structured is the way it must be."

"That's just how it is, Joe," she said softly. "I've accepted that."

Joe nodded, his mind racing.

Think, Dillon, he ordered himself. He honestly didn't know if he was falling in love with Polly, but he sure as hell wanted a chance to find out. He would not, could not, turn and walk out of that apartment, acknowledging the fact that he'd never see Polly Chapman again.

But he was a veteran of etched-in-stone thinking. He'd refused to budge from his theory that living in the ghetto was the best way to relate to the kids in the neighborhood. For years he'd turned a deaf ear to everyone's arguments that he was overdoing his dedication to the students of Abraham Lincoln High School.

It had taken a solid whop in the head in the form of

what Debbie and Jerome had said to make him come to his stubborn senses.

Talking, pleading, attempting to reason with Polly about the possibility that she might have more in her future if it was meant to be, wasn't going to cut it. It would take actions, not words.

So think, Dillon.

"All right, Polly," he said. "As difficult as this is for me to accept, I know I have to respect your beliefs."

Polly blinked. "You do?"

Joe dropped his hands from her face and Polly instantly missed the warmth of the gentle caress. Joe took a step backward and raised both hands.

"I won't touch you again," he said.

"You won't?" she said. Never again? Oh, dear, dear, that was terrible, so incredibly sad, so... No, no, it had to be this way. It really did. "Well, I...um...well, thank you." She would *not* cry. She'd never speak to herself again if she cried. "I appreciate your understanding."

"Certainly. You're welcome." Joe sighed, making the sound as dramatic as he could. "We'll just never know what this was that's happening between us, what we might have had together, but so be it."

"Like easy come, easy go?" Polly said, her voice gaining volume with each word.

"No," Joe said quickly. "This isn't easy for me, believe me, but I'm a man who deals in reality and you have delivered a heavy-duty dose of it. Facts are facts and, I repeat, so be it."

"Oh," Polly said, in a small voice.

"The thing is..." Joe said thoughtfully, staring up at the ceiling.

"Yes?" she said, leaning slightly toward him.

Joe looked at her again. "I'm about to become a

member of middle-class America. I've never been there before. I've lived in the world of ridiculously rich, then shifted to bare-bones poor. Middle-class is a total mystery to me, and I need help here, *your* help.''

"To do what?'' Polly said, eyeing him warily.

"I want to buy a house, furniture, a dog.'' Joe shrugged. "I don't have a clue as to where to begin. Who do I ask for assistance? Celine? Buffy? In a flash they'd have me in a house big enough for an army. They have their furniture custom designed, for Pete's sake. I can't afford that on a teacher's salary. I refuse to touch my other source of money, so I need your help.''

"But...''

"Look, we're mature adults. What we do here is back up our relationship to being friends, buddies.''

"Buddies?'' Polly said, more in the form of a squeak.

"Sure,'' he said, smiling brightly. "It's simply a matter of obtaining the proper mind-set. Emotions not nurtured just...'' he wiggled one hand in the air, "...fade into oblivion. No problem. So! Polly, my pal, will you help me select a house, furniture, give me the benefit of your expertise with animals in selecting my dog?''

"You're kidding. This is the craziest thing I've ever heard.''

"It is not. It's right on the mark. You have the knowledge I'm lacking. We've established the new boundaries of our relationship, per your personal desires. As mature adults, we put our emotions in the proper slot. You *are* a mature adult, aren't you?''

"Well, of course, I am,'' Polly said. "You're getting insulting again.''

"I'm making my point. This plan is perfect. There isn't one thing wrong with it. Right?''

"I guess so, but...''

"Great. Okay, I'm going to hit the road. I think I'll round up some boxes and start packing my stuff in my house down there by Lincoln. That way I'll be ready to roll when we find the place I should buy. I'll contact a real estate agent and get back to you when there are houses to look at." He turned and started toward the door. "See ya."

"Joe, wait."

He stopped and looked at Polly over one shoulder.

"Yes?" he said pleasantly.

"I...that is...this really isn't a good...but...oh, drat, I'm so confused I can't think straight, let alone string sensible words together."

"You'll be fine as soon as you do your mind-set shift thing. Guaranteed. Bye...buddy."

Polly raised one finger and opened her mouth to speak again, but in the next instant Joe was gone. She stared at the door, finally realized her mouth was still open and snapped it shut. She sank onto the sofa in a heap, wearily aware that her mind was a completely muddled mess.

Joe slid behind the wheel of his car, pulled the door shut, then leaned his head back on the seat.

Man, he thought, he was exhausted, felt as though he'd run ten miles at breakneck speed. He had been mentally scrambling for the words, the plan, the proposal, he'd presented to Polly.

He'd pulled it off, by golly, by blathering like an idiot, not giving Polly an opportunity to digest what he was saying, nor think it through.

Damn, he was good, a near-genius at times.

Joe frowned.

Of course, there was always the chance that Polly would come out of the fog he'd inflicted on her and refuse to go along. Well, he'd tackle that if it happened. He'd hit on her conscience, her basic goodness, her sense of right and wrong, of having agreed to help him, so how could she justify breaking her promise?

Joe straightened and pushed the car key into the ignition.

Buddies? Pals? Cripes, that was asinine. He wouldn't be allowed, by his own set-in-motion plan, to touch Polly, hold her, make sweet, beautiful love with her. He'd be a dying man every time he was with her.

Well, to use the phrase that was really beginning to get on his nerves...so be it.

But he'd take a page out of Polly's book and look at the bright side of this nonsensical situation. He was determined to, and he would have, the answers to the questions plaguing him about Polly.

And Polly? Well, she just might get some answers to questions she didn't believe she was eligible to ask.

"So be it," Joe said decisively, then turned the key.

As he drove away, he was smiling.

Nine

It was a weary Polly Chapman who reported to Dogwood Veterinary Clinic the next morning. She hadn't slept well, had tossed and turned, then had disturbing, nonsensical dreams when she managed to doze.

Her mind, Polly thought dismally, just wouldn't turn off. It kept replaying the last scene with Joe in her living room, echoing his words over and over.

She entered one of the back rooms, hung up her sweater and purse, then put her brown lunch sack in the refrigerator. She stopped at Jazzy's cage, where the macaw was busily indulging in some big, juicy grapes.

"Pals? Buddies?" Polly said to the bird. "Is that crazy, Jazzy? Is Joe Dillon totally nuts?"

"Joe," Jazzy squawked. "Give me the bird, Joe, and a bottle of beer."

Polly rolled her eyes heavenward. "You're a big help. A bottle of beer isn't going to solve this dilemma. I need to know if I should agree to go along with Joe's plan. Well? Don't just sit there. Speak up."

"Polly want a cracker?" Jazzy said.

"No, I want an answer!"

"Goodness," Nancy Dogwood said, coming into the room. "You're not your usual sunny self this Monday morning, Polly. What do you need an answer to?"

"The question," Polly said, sighing. "Oh, ignore me, Nancy. I had a very strange weekend, to put it mildly." Glorious, too. Making love with Joe had been so exquisitely beautiful. "So much happened that I feel as though days, weeks, have gone by since I was here on Friday."

"You look tired," Nancy said, coming to where Polly stood by Jazzy's cage.

"I haven't slept worth diddly. I...oh, never mind. I'll be all right once I get busy here and can think about something other than what I'm thinking about."

Nancy frowned. "I've never seen you so frazzled. Would you like to talk about it? What's this question that you want an answer to?"

"Joe," Jazzy said. "Wanna snuggle, bunny?"

"Hush," Polly told the bird.

"Joe?" Nancy said. "Is our Jazzy turning into a psychic phenomenon? Is Joe Dillon the cause of your upset, Polly?"

"Yes, but it's very complicated. Thank you for the offer, but I'd rather not discuss it."

"Are you beginning to care for Joe?" Nancy said.

"Well, I... Well, yes, but I don't want to talk about it."

"Does he care for you?"

Polly nodded.

"Oh, isn't that splendid?" Nancy said, beaming.

"No!" Polly said, more in the form of a wail.

"Oh," Nancy said, blinking in surprise at Polly's outburst. "I'm sorry. It certainly sounded splendid to *me*."

"Well, it's not," Polly said, then sniffled. "Oh, I'm a wreck. I have to get to work before I totally lose it."

"If you decide you want to talk about it, I'll be happy to listen," Nancy said. "The truth be known, I'm dying of curiosity."

"Mmm," Polly said, frowning.

"All right, to work," Nancy said. "Oh, there's a manicurist from an exclusive pet grooming boutique coming by this morning to do Pookie the poodle's nails."

"What?" Polly said, her eyes widening.

"It's true," Nancy said, laughing. "There was a message on the answering machine when I got in this morning."

"For Pete's sake," Polly said, "that is ridiculous. That dog has gourmet dog food and steak from a fancy restaurant, real gems on her collar—and now she's having her nails done by an overpaid pet manicurist?"

Nancy shrugged. "Her owners can afford it."

"That's not the point," Polly said. "Nancy, I met a couple of kids this weekend who plan to be married when they graduate from high school.

"Debbie, the bride-to-be, said that someday, maybe, she and Jerome might actually have their own furniture. She had a wistful tone of voice when she said it, as though she knew it might never happen."

Nancy frowned. "What does that have to do with Pookie's meals, her nails?"

"It's just so out of balance, or something," Polly said, pressing her fingertips to her now throbbing temples. "Yes, pets are members of a person's family but... Did it ever occur to people like Pookie's owners that there are deserving souls out there who need some help to make something of their lives?''

''It's not our place to question how our clients spend their money, Polly.'' Nancy paused. ''You've never expressed such a judgmental attitude before. You laughed yourself silly last year when the violin player came to serenade the pouting Doberman we were boarding. Gracious, just what did happen to you over the weekend?''

''I dealt with people, instead of pets,'' Polly said quietly. ''Living, breathing people, with hopes and dreams. I touched their lives and they touched mine.''

''And one of those people was Joe Dillon.''

''Yes,'' Polly whispered. ''One of those people was Joe.''

Joe pocketed the piece of paper that Mark Jackson had handed to him as the two men stood in Mark's office at Lincoln.

''Thanks, Mark,'' Joe said, ''I appreciate the help.''

''That Realtor is sharp,'' the principal said. ''She'll do a good job. I'm happy for you, Joe. It's time you had a decent house.''

''You knew, didn't you?'' Joe said. ''You knew that the students here at Lincoln thought I was crazy to live in this neighborhood.''

Mark nodded. ''There was no purpose to be served in telling you. I'd heard your stand on the subject enough times to realize that I'd be wasting my breath trying to get through to you.''

''Yeah,'' Joe said, nodding, ''you're right. I wouldn't have listened.''

''Well, thank goodness for Polly Chapman,'' Mark said, smiling. ''You're actually going to have a life beyond Lincoln, which is the way it should be.'' He paused and raised his eyebrows. "Could it be that the ever famous Bird Lady is going to be a part of that new existence?"

"Who knows?" Joe said, sighing. "But I'll tell you this, Mark. If I don't get some answers soon to the questions hammering at me, I'm going to go right out of my ever lovin' mind."

"Ah, women." Mark laughed. "They can cut the biggest, strongest guy right off at the knees, bless their hearts."

"This isn't funny, Mark. My mind is mush." Joe turned and started away. "I'm going to concentrate on my dog before I blow a circuit in my brain."

Mark frowned as Joe left the office.

"Joe doesn't have a dog," the principal said to no one, then chuckled. "You're going down for the count, Dillon. The Bird Lady has gotcha."

During the next three days, as Polly waited to hear from Joe, she began to formulate a plan that would, she told herself in her best Pollyanna fashion, save her teetering sanity.

On Thursday evening, while indulging in a leisurely bubble bath, Polly clicked the last piece of the puzzle of her plan into place and nodded.

She leaned her head back on the rim of the tub and sighed with self-satisfaction.

She was all set, she mused. She'd sifted, sorted and mulled to her heart's content, and was now calm and in control.

The Plan, which she now envisioned in her mind as having a capital *P*, was brilliant, if she did say so herself. Yes, okay, she'd admittedly borrowed a bit of Joe's philosophy, his statement that emotions not nurtured just faded into oblivion. Fine.

She had two choices. She could refuse to see Joe Dillon again, or she could go along with his plan. Did he use a mental capital *P,* too? she wondered, absently bursting soap bubbles with one fingertip.

Anyway, she rambled on in her mind, she'd made her decision. She'd agree to go house hunting and furniture shopping with Joe. She'd spend, in fact, as much time as feasibly possible in his company. As his buddy. His pal. His friend.

The more hours she was in that role, the faster the romantic memories of Joe…the kisses, caresses, the soft smiles and wondrous lovemaking…would fade. Not nurtured—the emotions stemming from those special, beautiful moments would disappear, poof, be gone.

When Joe's mission of finding a nice, middle-class home to buy, then selecting furniture to put in it, was completed, she could walk away from him and his new life without a backward glance or a broken heart.

Right? Right.

"Look at the bright side," Polly said aloud. "I even get to help Joe pick out a dog. This will be fun."

Yes, the Plan was good, very good. It would be much easier to obtain, and maintain, the status of Joe's buddy while in his never-touching-her-again presence. To attempt to forget him in solitary confinement could very well result in sensuous memories nibbling away at her resolve to forget him.

"Well-done, Polly," she said. "Okay, Mr. Dillon, I'm ready to go house shopping. Bring 'em on. Call me on the phone and say you're ready to roll."

At that exact moment the telephone rang, causing Polly to jerk upward in the bathtub at the sound of the

sudden noise she'd just mentally demanded to hear. She
pulled the plug in her bath, then stepped out onto the
mat on the floor, reaching for a towel at the same time.

Wrapped in the towel, dripping water and shivering,
she hurried into the bedroom to snatch up the receiver
to the telephone on the nightstand.

"Hello?" she said breathlessly.

"Polly? Joe. You sound out of breath. Did I disturb
you?"

"No, not really. I was taking a bubble bath."

"Oh," he said.

A bubble bath? he thought. Polly was talking to him
while wearing nothing more than maybe a towel? Her
skin would be moist, dewy and have the aroma of some
enticing, feminine bath oil. Her face would be flushed a
pretty pink from the heat of the water and...cripes, this
woman didn't play fair.

"Well, I won't keep you long," Joe said. "I wouldn't
want you to catch a cold."

"I *am* a tad chilly," Polly returned.

Joe's voice was so rich, deep and masculine, she
thought dreamily. She adored his voice, could listen to
him talk for hours on end. And when he laughed, or
chuckled? Oh, mercy, her bones dissolved.

A shiver coursed through Polly and she clutched the
damp towel tighter.

If Joe was there in that room, she mused on, she
wouldn't be cold for long. No, by golly, she'd be very
warm, very *hot,* very quickly. *Polly Chapman, shame on
you.*

"Polly?"

"What? Oh. Yes, I'm here, Joe."

"The agent I contacted has lined up four houses for

me to see on Saturday. Is that a convenient day for you?''

"Yes, it's fine.''

"Great. I'll pick you up at nine Saturday morning. I want to get an early start because I have a game to coach that night at Lincoln.''

"There's a basketball game on Saturday night? I'd like to go. I had such a super time at the one I attended, and I could see Debbie and Jerome again and...''

"No.''

"No? I can't see Debbie and Jerome? Why not?''

"No, you can't come to the game,'' Joe said. "I don't want you alone in this neighborhood. You'd have to park heaven only knows where, then walk to the school. No. Absolutely not.''

Polly narrowed her eyes. "I beg your pardon, Mr. Dillon, but you are not my keeper.'' Or my lover. Not anymore. Oh, dear, dear, that was really quite depressing. "As my *buddy,* my *friend,* you may offer advice, which I may, or may not, choose to follow.''

"You're being difficult,'' Joe said. "Use some common sense. You wouldn't be safe in this neighborhood at night. Hell, you wouldn't be safe in broad daylight. You don't need *me* to tell you that.''

"Hmm,'' Polly said thoughtfully. "Okay, try this. Give Debbie and Jerome my telephone number and ask them to please call me. I'll arrange to meet them somewhere, take them with me to park, then the three of us will walk to the school together.''

Joe sighed. "Yes, okay, you win.''

"I hope the Grizzlies win on Saturday night. We're still undefeated. That is so terrific.''

"The team we're playing Saturday is tough,'' Joe said. "They have a center who is six feet seven. The only saving grace is that he gets called for traveling a lot. I think he trips over his own big feet.''

Polly laughed. "I'll have my work cut out for me then. You know, keeping the referees informed about when that big kid travels. I got so excited at the last game, I went nuts. I wouldn't blame Debbie and Jerome if they didn't want to sit with me again.''

"Oh, I'm sure they'll be glad to see you," Joe said. "I...well, I enjoyed catching glimpses of you giving your all at the game. I was glad you were there, Polly.''

"Thank you, Joe," she said softly. "I was glad I was there, too.''

Neither spoke for a long moment. The silence on the telephone line seemed to crackle with yearning.

Joe cleared his throat.

"Yes, well," he said, "you must be freezing. I'll pick you up at nine on Saturday. Goodbye, Polly.''

"Goodbye," she said, then realized she'd just bid the dial tone farewell.

She replaced the receiver, then stomped back toward the bathroom.

"Friends, buddies, pals," she chanted, in time to her marching feet. "Pals, buddies, friends.''

Joe dropped the telephone receiver into place, then glowered into space.

So far, so good, he thought. Polly was going to go along with the plan to help him find a house.

What *he* needed to do was get a grip on his libido. Just hearing her voice and imagining her wrapped in a skimpy towel had caused heated desire to tie him in knots.

Lust, he decided. It would be there when he was in close proximity to Polly because he was a normal, healthy man and Polly was a very desirable woman. He'd simply have to maintain control over his raging testosterone when he was with her.

Lust had nothing to do with emotions, with the un-answered questions he had.

"Lust," he said aloud. "Lust?"

Boy, that was a tacky word. It was so crude, cold and carnal. It just didn't fit the image in his mind, the mem-ories, of making love with Polly. Emotions *had* been intertwined with the physical when they'd made love...incredible love, really sensational.

His little hummingbird was a very passionate woman who gave of herself in total abandon. While in his em-brace, she trusted him completely, making him feel pro-tective and possessive.

And caring.

Caring very, very much.

Joe lunged to his feet and started forward, nearly fall-ing over a packing box that he'd forgotten he'd put in the center of the floor of the small living room.

He went into the kitchen, opened the refrigerator, stared unseeing at the offerings within, then slammed the door closed.

"All right, Dillon," he said, dragging a restless hand through his hair. "Think this through. Just stay calm, in control, and think."

If he had admitted to himself that meshing his body with Polly's had not been basic lust, had not been merely sex, but had been making love, was that important?

Was there an answer, somewhere in that information, to one of his questions regarding the depths of his feel-ings for Polly?

If a man was acutely aware that he had *made* love

with a woman, did that indicate that he was *falling* in love with said woman?

"Well, hell," he said. "I don't know. Why don't I know?"

All he'd managed to do, he thought, with self-disgust, was add another question to the towering stack already plaguing him.

"Nice going, Dillon, you dolt," he muttered. "Go pack a box."

Friday dragged by slowly for Polly. The days at the clinic seemed endless, as she found herself glancing often at the clock on the wall. A clock, she was convinced, that had stopped ticking.

She was edgy, had to bite her tongue to keep from making derogatory remarks about the attention she was expected to lavish on the pampered pets being boarded at the Dogwood Veterinary Clinic.

The only look-at-the-bright-side event had been a telephone call from Debbie, who said that she and Jerome were really looking forward to attending the basketball game with their new friend Polly. They made arrangements to meet Polly at a convenience store several blocks from the school on Saturday night.

Late Friday afternoon, Polly rolled her eyes in exasperation as she read *Goodnight Moon* for the third time in a row to a Siamese cat.

Had anyone ever read *Goodnight Moon* to Debbie or Jerome when they were little children? she wondered. Had anyone tucked them in at night, made them feel safe and loved?

Did parents who were struggling to survive in the ghetto have the physical and emotional energy for such things as stories and hugs at the end of a day?

"My goodness, Polly," Nancy said, coming into the room, "I've never heard *Goodnight Moon* sound so gloomy. You're going to give that poor cat nightmares."

Polly snapped the book closed and frowned.

"Nancy," she said, "this is ridiculous. I'm reading a story to a cat, for heaven's sake. I have more to offer than this. I worked very hard for my degree, have skills that— Oh, I'm sorry. Please forget I just said all that."

Nancy pulled a chair close to Polly and sat down.

"Polly," she said, concern evident in her voice and on her face, "you're not as happy working here as you once were, are you?"

Polly traced the letters of the title of the book in her lap with a fingertip, then finally met Nancy's troubled gaze.

"No," Polly said, "I guess I'm not. Suddenly I'm having a difficult time justifying the excesses lavished on some of these animals by their owners. There are so many people in need in this world that I'm finding it harder and harder to see the humor in what these pets are continually given."

Nancy nodded slowly. "Are you going to leave us?"

"I don't know, Nancy. I'm very confused about a great many things right now. Besides, I can't just think of myself. My brother and sister are counting on the financial help I give them." Polly managed to produce a small smile. "You pay me very well to read stories to cats."

"Robert and I don't want to lose you," Nancy said. "You're part of the family here. Let me talk to Robert over the weekend and see if we can come up with a solution of some kind that will work for all of us. Okay?"

"Yes, of course. I apologize for causing you any upset, Nancy."

"There's no need to apologize. I'm glad we had this
talk. Now, go home and have a marvelous weekend. Do
you have fun things scheduled?"

"Tomorrow is jam-packed," Polly said. "Will it be
fun? I don't have a clue."

By the time Joe was due to arrive the next morning,
Polly had given herself so many stern lectures regarding
the necessity to distance herself emotionally from Joe
while she was with him, she was thoroughly worn-out
from the sound of her own mental voice.

"Just shut up and keep your act together," she said
aloud.

Joe's knock on the door came at exactly nine o'clock.
Polly answered the summons with a bright smile while
ignoring the swarm of butterflies whizzing around in her
stomach.

"Hi," she said, stepping back to allow Joe to enter
the living room. Oh, hello, Joe Dillon, in jeans and black
knit shirt, looking so male and magnificent it was sinful.
"How are you this morning?"

"Fine," he said, nodding. Cute as a button. Polly
Chapman in jeans and a red-and-white striped sport top
was...well, cute as a button. A button he wanted to haul
into his arms and kiss...right now. *Forget it, Dillon.*
"Ready to go?"

"Sure." Polly picked up her purse. "I'm all set."

"We're meeting the real estate agent, Sue Simpson,
at the first house on the list," Joe said, as they left the
apartment.

"And she has four houses for you...us...to see?"

"Yep."

"Oh."

Dandy, Polly thought, as Joe drove away from the curb. Now what did they talk about? She was suddenly afraid to start a conversation in fear of addressing a subject that was beyond the boundaries of Polly-and-Joe-are-pals. Oh, dear, dear, this was very complicated and so stressful.

"Nice weather today," Joe said, breaking the heavy silence that had settled over the interior of the car.

"Yes. Yes, it's quite warm for this time of year, isn't it?"

"Mmm," he said, frowning.

Lame, Joe thought in self-disgust. He'd already resorted to discussing the weather? Cripes. He'd started to ask Polly if she'd slept well and was full of pep in regard to tromping around looking at houses. It seemed like an innocent enough topic until he'd opened his mouth to speak.

Then suddenly the question of Polly's sleep conjured up images of Polly's bed and the fantastic lovemaking they'd shared there.

Damn. Being buddies with Polly was obviously going to be very hard work. But this was the only way he could be assured that he could be in close proximity to her, have a fighting chance to get the answers to his questions. Therefore, once again, so be it.

They drove the remaining miles to the first house in total silence.

Sue Simpson was a plump, cheerful woman in her fifties. She greeted Polly and Joe with a smile and a listing of the house they were about to enter for each of them.

Within two minutes, both Joe and Polly shook their

heads in negative response to what they saw. The house was paneled throughout in dark wood, causing the rooms to appear small and dreary.

"Then off we go," Sue said pleasantly. "Follow my car to number two."

Number two was a dud. The owners had knocked out the majority of the interior walls to make a loft effect, resulting in more of a furniture warehouse with very little privacy.

House number three needed a new roof, all new appliances, and something done immediately about the bright orange carpeting.

"Oh, dear, dear," Polly said, "this is very discouraging."

"Not really," Sue said. "I'm simply giving you a variety to view so you have an idea of what is on the market. Onward and upward. I saved the best for last."

"My house down by Lincoln is starting to look good," Joe said, under his breath.

Polly choked on a burst of laughter she attempted, but failed, to curb.

Then there it was…house number four.

"Oh, my," Polly said, as the trio stood on the sidewalk in front of the structure.

"Now we're getting somewhere," Joe said.

The house was a ranch-style redbrick with two tall mulberry trees in the front yard. There was a front porch large enough to hold lawn furniture, and the front door boasted a rectangular stained-glass panel.

"This house is empty," Sue said. "The owners have moved to Alaska and are eager to sell. You can roam around inside all you wish. I'll keep out of your way, but I'll be available to answer your questions."

Inside the house, Polly knew she was smiling, but she couldn't help herself.

Perfect, she thought. It was absolutely perfect.

Nice, Joe thought. This was it, no doubt about it.

The rooms were large and glowing with bright sunlight. The carpeting was milk-chocolate brown, the kitchen appliances a sparkling white.

There was a bay window with cushioned seats, creating a charming breakfast nook. The master bedroom and bath were on one side of the house, with two bedrooms and bath on the other. A flagstone fireplace in the living room was edged by floor-to-ceiling oak bookcases.

"What do you think?" Joe asked Polly.

"It's wonderful, Joe," she said, smiling up at him.

He nodded. "Yes, I agree. I'm going to go check out the backyard."

"Okay."

As Joe disappeared, Polly wandered down the hallway containing the two bedrooms and a bathroom. She stood in the doorway to one of the good-size, sunny rooms.

This is the nursery, she thought. One wall could be papered with perky bunnies, or snuggly teddy bears, or laughing clowns, with a matching border print edging the top of the other walls.

There was space for a crib, changing table, bookcase and toy box, and a special place near the window for a rocking chair.

Her rocking chair, the one now in her apartment, the one her mother had spent endless hours in over the years rocking her precious babies. The rocking chair that she, Polly Chapman, would settle into, holding the miracle, the child, created by lovemaking shared with Joe Dillon.

Only vaguely aware that she was moving, Polly

walked forward slowly, stopping in the middle of the room in a warm, golden circle of sunlight.

The images in her mind of the cozy nursery were so vivid, so real, it was as though she could reach out and touch the rocking chair, the pristine white crib, the matching changing table, the brightly colored toys in the toy box.

She felt strange, as though she had floated outside herself and was watching from afar as the baby's nursery became a reality.

This was the luxury of dreaming, Polly thought hazily. This was allowing herself to listen to her heart, instead of her Pollyanna head. This was giving full rein to hopes and dreams, yearnings of having a home, a husband and children.

This was embracing the realization that those dreams centered on Joe.

Joe, who would share this place with her, transform it from a house into a home.

Joe, who would be her husband.

Joe, who would be the father of the baby snuggled under a fluffy blanket in the crib.

This was the unraveling of the tangled maze of confusion in her mind to reveal the truth.

She was in love with Joe Dillon.

Polly smiled. In her dreamlike state she welcomed that love, savored the warmth of it as it swept throughout her, matching the warmth of the sunlight on her tingling skin.

She held out her arms and turned around slowly, drinking in the sight of the beautiful nursery, hearing the baby's gurgling laughter, feeling Joe's presence so close to her as they gazed lovingly at their child.

"Teddy bears," she heard herself say from a faraway

place. "Yes, Joe and I will decorate this nursery in fuzzy teddy bears, each ready to give a hug.

"Music. Oh, yes, we must have music for our baby. A teddy bear musical mobile hanging over the crib, and a music box on the dresser.

"Joe will be a wonderful father. We'll be such a happy family. Love and laughter will fill this home to overflowing. I love you, little baby, and, oh, how I love you, Joe Dillon."

Joe sank back against the wall next to the open doorway of the room where Polly had spoken in a whisper-soft, reverent voice. His heart thundered and a trickle of sweat ran down his chest.

My God, he thought, Polly Chapman loved him, was honestly and truly in love with him.

She was envisioning this as *their* home, was standing in a room she saw as a nursery for *their* child.

Polly was giving way to her innermost hopes and dreams, which she'd stated firmly she mustn't do, couldn't, wouldn't do.

Polly loved him.

Was that wonderful? Was that terrible and terrifying? Damn it, why didn't he know?

He couldn't go on like this.

He had to have the answers to his tormenting questions.

Joe pushed himself away from the wall and stepped into the open doorway to the room.

"Polly," he said quietly.

Polly jerked in surprise at the sudden sound of Joe's voice, blinked, then frowned.

"Yes?" she said, shaking her head slightly.

"The backyard will be great for a dog."

"A what?" she said. "Oh, a dog. Yes, the dog you're going to get."

"Do you really like the house?"

"I love it," she said, managing to produce a small smile.

And I love you, Joe Dillon, she thought. Oh, dear heaven, how had that happened? When had she lost control of her emotions, lost her heart to Joe?

He mustn't know how she felt. Oh, dear, dear, no! Her hopes, dreams, her love for Joe, were being pushed away into oblivion, now, right now. They weren't hers to have. She had to think of Ted and Megan, not herself. And she had to get out of this room.

"I think this house will be perfect for you, Joe," she said, "and for your new middle-class life-style." She paused. "I'm going to look at the backyard."

Polly hurried across the room, edged past Joe at the doorway, then nearly ran down the hall.

Joe watched her go, then turned again to sweep his gaze over the sunny room.

Teddy bears? his mind hammered. A baby created by lovemaking shared with Polly, his wife? Music and laughter and love within these walls?

Joe dragged trembling hands down his face.

Was all of that what he wanted? What *did* he want? *What did he really, truly want?*

Ten

Having been deposited by Joe back at her apartment, Polly spent the afternoon cleaning everything in sight, which included things that didn't need cleaning.

She alternated between sniffling and struggling not to cry in despair, and mentally raging at herself for not having maintained tight control over her emotions, the depths of her feelings, for Joe.

She was in love for the first time in her life, and she was miserable.

She had slipped into the glorious arena of hopes and dreams where she didn't belong, had no right to be, and had a painfully aching heart to show for her transgression.

As she nibbled at a dinner she had no appetite for, she realized she did not want to attend the basketball game at Lincoln that night. She had no choice but to go, as the plan to meet Debbie and Jerome was set in motion.

But, oh, dear, dear, she thought frantically, how could she sit in that noisy gym, staring at Joe Dillon—the man she loved? When the final buzzer sounded to end the game, the blaring noise would also be signaling the last time she could see the man who had stolen her heart.

She could not, she knew, go furniture shopping with Joe for the enchanting, picture-perfect house for which he had submitted an offer to purchase. She couldn't bear to walk through those sunny rooms again, imagining Joe living there...without her.

Polly glanced at her watch, then got up from the table. After she'd straightened up the kitchen from preparing dinner, took a shower and changed her clothes, it would be time to leave to meet Debbie and Jerome.

Look at the bright side, Pollyanna, she told herself gloomily. At least she could escape from her apartment for a few hours, get a reprieve from the heavy, dark cloud hanging over her head within these walls.

After dropping Polly off at her apartment, then meeting with Sue Simpson at the Realtor's office to sign the necessary papers to make an offer on the house, Joe headed for home.

Halfway to the south side of town, he felt a strange emotional tug, a pull, in the opposite direction. He turned at the next intersection and drove all the way back to the house he intended to buy.

After parking in the driveway of the redbrick structure, Joe cut across the lawn, settled onto the porch steps, then swept his gaze over the well-kept homes on the street.

A breeze whispered through the leaves of the two

mulberry trees in the front yard of the would-hopefully-be Dillon residence, creating a soft, calming hum that Joe allowed to float over him with a gentle touch.

He narrowed his eyes, envisioning the interior of the house, and began to mentally put furniture in the large, sunny rooms.

He filled the tall bookcases in the living room with books and knickknacks, placed matching chairs by the fireplace, included lamps and oak tables, and a comfortable, puffy sofa.

In the master bedroom was a king-size bed, oak nightstands, a dresser and chest of drawers. Two sets of towels hung in the master bathroom.

Joe took a deep breath, let it out, then took himself, in his mind's eye, down the hallway leading to the extra bedrooms. He stopped in the doorway to the room where he'd found Polly when he'd returned to the house from the backyard.

The room was empty.

Then slowly, very slowly, as though a heavy fog were lifting, he saw a baby crib that was…yes, it was white, with a white changing table, brightly colored toys, and there were the teddy bears. He heard music, a sweet lullaby tinkling through the air from a delicate music box set on top of a white dresser.

He saw Polly standing by the crib, and he was right next to her, his arm encircling her shoulders to tuck her close and safely by his side as they gazed into the crib.

And Joe Dillon knew, at long last he knew, the answers to his questions.

As he sat there on the steps of the house that would become a home filled with love and laughter, he knew.

He was in love with Polly Chapman.

And he was consumed by the greatest joy and the

greatest sense of inner peace that he had ever experienced in his entire life.

"Yes," Joe said quietly, giving way to a smile.

He got to his feet and punched one fist in the air.

"Yes!" he shouted.

But as he drove toward home, his smile changed into a deep frown.

Polly loved him, he thought. She was truly in love with him, which was fantastic. He did, however, have a rough road ahead as far as convincing her to become his wife, to spend the rest of their lives together, raise beautiful babies in the music-filled, teddy bear nursery.

Yeah, he had his work cut out for him, all right, because Polly Chapman didn't allow herself to have hopes and dreams. She was totally focused on her responsibility of helping put her brother and sister through college.

Polly felt, as he once had, that there was no room in her life for love, marriage, home and family.

Well, it was because of Polly's caring enough about him to tell him what Debbie and Jerome had said about crazy Coach Dillon living in the ghetto that he had changed, grown, broadened his world.

It was because of Polly, his love for her, that he wanted it all.

"The battle is on, Ms. Chapman," Joe said aloud, narrowing his eyes. "I'm going to win. I have to. Oh, man, I just have to."

A future without Polly was unthinkable. Living in his new house without Polly there to help make it a real home was unacceptable. A life without his little hummingbird would be too stark, empty, chillingly lonely.

He would do whatever it took to convince Polly to let him take over the financial obligation to her siblings. He would do whatever it took to give Polly the hopes and dreams she was keeping at bay.

Polly Chapman would be his.

With a decisive nod, Joe forced himself to shift mental gears into his coaching mode to prepare for the tough basketball game to be played that night.

With each passing mile that Polly drove toward the south side of town and her rendezvous with Debbie and Jerome, the more tense she became. Her grip on the steering wheel of the rattling van was so tight, her knuckles turned white from the pressure.

She couldn't do this, she thought frantically. She couldn't sit in that gym, staring at Joe, knowing that although she was in love with him, they had no chance of a future together. Even if Joe was, maybe, perhaps, falling in love with her, a forever and ever together was not theirs to have.

No, she just couldn't do it. It was too sad, too heart-breaking. It was a pea-soup green bicycle instead of a candy-apple red one magnified tenfold in crushing dis-appointment.

"I can't go to the basketball game," Polly whispered, struggling against threatening tears. "I just can't."

When Polly pulled into the parking lot of the desig-nated convenience store, she saw Debbie and Jerome, who immediately smiled, waved, then ran to the van as Polly pressed on the brake. Debbie opened the creaking, passenger side door.

"Hi, Polly," she said, beaming. "It's so great to see you. Say hi, Jerome."

"Hi, Jerome," he said, then hooted with laughter. "Sorry. I couldn't resist. Hi, Polly."

"Hi," she said quietly.

Oh, look at them, she thought. Debbie and Jerome were so young, so vitally alive, so happy. They had hopes and dreams of a future together, marriage, a wonderful little baby. They were determined to leave the ghetto, move uptown and, maybe, someday, have their very own furniture. With a dose of realism firmly in place to keep them steady, they were going to have it all.

"Debbie, Jerome," Polly said, "I didn't have any way to contact you, so I drove down here to tell you that I'm not feeling well. I'll drive you over to the school, but then I'm heading home to bed."

"You're sick?" Debbie said, frowning. "Wow. That's a bummer."

"Does Coach Dillon know you're not coming to the game?" Jerome said.

"No," Polly said. "You can tell him for me. Just say I caught a bug, or whatever. Get in and I'll drop you off at Lincoln."

The pair slid onto the lumpy front seat and Polly pressed on the gas.

"You don't look sick," Debbie said, staring at Polly. "Well, you're kind of pale, I guess, but...did you and Coach Dillon have a fight or something? Is that why you're not coming to the game?"

Polly shook her head. Debbie leaned closer.

"Yep, that's it, all right," Debbie said, nodding. "You're ready to let go with the waterworks. What did that rotten man do?"

"Debbie, please," Polly said, swallowing past the lump in her throat. "I have the flu. Okay?"

Debbie slouched back against the seat and folded her arms over her breasts.

"No, it is *not* okay," she said. "You need to march

into that gym and give Coach Dillon what for, a hefty piece of your mind for upsetting you like this.''

''Debbie,'' Jerome said, ''jeez, quit messin' in their business.''

''I know the rules, Jerome,'' Debbie said, ''but this is different.''

''Yeah, right,'' Jerome said, shaking his head.

''It is,'' Debbie said. ''Polly and Coach Dillon are in love with each other and…''

''Debbie,'' Polly interrupted, ''I never said one word about being in love with Coach Dillon, or his being in love with me.''

''Well, I wasn't born yesterday,'' Debbie said. ''I have eyes, you know. Any fool can tell how you two feel about each other. Now you've gone and had a fight. You've got to square off against the big dolt, Polly. Men are just so dumb at times. State your program and get on with the kissing and making up. Tell her, Jerome.''

''*I'm* not messin' in their business,'' Jerome said.

''You are worthless, Jerome,'' Debbie said. ''Polly, are you listening to me?''

''Here's the school,'' Polly said. ''There's a car on my bumper. Out you go.''

''But…'' Debbie said.

Jerome opened the door and grabbed Debbie's hand.

''Out,'' he said. ''Bye, Polly.''

''But…'' Debbie said, as Jerome pulled her across the seat.

Jerome slammed the door and Polly drove away as quickly as possible. Two tears slid down her pale cheeks.

Inside the noisy Multipurpose Building that was being used that night as a gymnasium, the players of both basketball teams were going through warm-up routines. A steady stream of students poured through the double doors and settled onto the bleachers.

Joe stood at the far end of the building, chatting with the coach from the opposing team. Joe glanced often at his players, which allowed him to keep track of who was coming into the gym.

When he saw Debbie enter with Jerome right behind her, Joe's heart quickened as he watched for Polly to bring up the rear. But Polly didn't appear.

Where was she? he thought, feeling his muscles tense. Where in the hell was Polly? Debbie was headed straight for him, looking as though she were ready to murder someone. What was going on here?

"Excuse me, Jimmy," Joe said, to the other coach. "I need to speak with a couple of students of mine."

"Sure thing," Jimmy said. "It was good talking to you, Joe."

Joe nodded, then walked in front of the bleachers to meet Debbie and Jerome.

"Where's Polly?" Joe said, as the trio stopped their trek.

"I need to speak with you, Coach," Debbie said. "Privately."

"All right," Joe said. "Come over by the locker room door."

At the designated place, Joe turned with a frown to face Debbie and Jerome.

"Where's Polly?" he repeated.

Jerome stared at a spot on the wall and rocked nervously back and forth on the balls of his feet. Debbie took a deep breath, let it out slowly, then planted her hands on her hips.

"Coach Dillon," she said, "I'm not speaking to you

as a student to a teacher, but as a woman to a man. Have you got that?''

Joe blinked in surprise, then nodded, realizing he'd been struck momentarily speechless.

''Good,'' Debbie said. ''Now then, listen up. Polly is my friend. She's Jerome's friend, too. She drove down here to tell us she was sick and couldn't come to the game. Well, she isn't sick. No way. She was working so hard at not crying, it just broke my heart.

''I figure that's your fault, Coach. Polly is really upset, and you must be the cause. If you two had a fight, then fix it, because a wonderful person like Polly shouldn't be sitting home alone crying her eyes out over a man. Not even a decent sort of man like you are. Men just aren't worth crying buckets over.''

''Hey,'' Jerome said, ''I resent that.''

''Hush, Jerome,'' she said. ''Coach, if you lose Polly Chapman because of something stupid you did, then you're dumber than a rock. It will be even more ridiculous than your living down here in the ghetto all these years when you didn't even have to. When this basketball game is over, you'd best get yourself to Polly's apartment and set things to rights. There. I've had my say. Goodbye, Coach. Come on, Jerome.''

Debbie stomped away. Jerome gave Joe a weak smile, shrugged, then hurried after Debbie.

Joe shook his head slightly, then splayed one hand on his stomach, feeling as though he'd just been punched in the gut.

Polly was upset? She'd been struggling not to cry when she'd told Debbie and Jerome she was too sick to attend the game? Crying because of him? What had *he* done to Polly to cause her tears?

Think, Dillon.

Okay. They'd both been rather quiet after leaving the house that Joe knew he intended to buy. The drive back to Polly's had been completed in nearly total silence, each apparently lost in their own thoughts.

His thoughts, he knew, had been centered on the maze of confusion in his mind. He had just discovered the truth of Polly's depths of feelings for him, knew she loved him. He'd still been scared spitless over the prospect of being loved, loving in return, getting married, having a family. He just didn't know at that point if that was what he wanted, didn't have the answers to his multitude of questions.

It hadn't been until he'd gone back to the house alone that he'd found his answers, knew he was in love with Polly, knew he wanted, needed it all...a lifetime of love and laughter with Polly Chapman.

He was now emotionally squared away, on track and determined to win the battle of chipping away at Polly's wall of settling for less than she deserved to have, of believing that she alone was responsible for the financial obligation to her brother and sister.

For each brick in that stubborn wall that he destroyed, he'd replace it with dreams that could be his and Polly's reality. Marriage. Home. Babies in a musical, teddy bear nursery. Forever. Together.

Yes.

Dandy, Joe thought dryly. He was painting pretty pictures in his mind, instead of concentrating on the immediate problem at hand.

Why was Polly crying?

The sermonette delivered by feisty Miss Debbie was disturbing, to say the least.

But then again...

Joe narrowed his eyes in concentration.

Maybe…yes, this was beginning to make sense. Polly's tears were caused by the fact that she'd acknowledged the truth, had admitted to herself that she was in love with him. *She* wanted it all, just as much as he did. Polly was crying because she couldn't envision her hopes and dreams possibly coming true.

The news flash that Polly Chapman was crying was terrific!

The buzzer blared, causing Joe to jerk in surprise and remember that he was in the gym at Lincoln and had a basketball game to coach.

He hurried to where his players were gathering in front of the bleachers.

"Okay, guys," he said to the boys, "this one is going to be very tough. A lot depends on how badly you want it. There's no doubt in *my* mind that a victory can be yours if you put everything you have into it."

Listen to your own words, Dillon, Joe told himself. The same held true for his entire future happiness with Polly.

Eleven

The Abraham Lincoln Grizzlies won the basketball game by three points, despite the less than inspired coaching on the part of Mr. Dillon.

In the locker room after the victory, Joe apologized to his team for the technical foul he'd received for signaling for a time-out when they had already used their allotted number.

"That's okay, Coach," Luis said. "We whipped their butts, even though they made the free throws from the technical. We figured, like, you know, you were thinking about your Bird Lady, seeing how she wasn't at the game tonight and all."

"Yes, well…um…" Joe said, then cleared his throat. "Hit the showers."

As he drove to Polly's apartment, Joe shook his head in a combined gesture of amazement and bewilderment.

Were all teenagers as savvy as those at Lincoln? he

wondered. Or were these streetwise kids more in tune to the adult world than the affluent, protected ones from the other side of town?

Debbie, Jerome, the basketball team…hell, the whole school, for all he knew…were aware that Coach Dillon had heart trouble over Polly Chapman.

"Now *that* is embarrassing," he said aloud, with a snort of self-disgust.

In the next instant Joe took a deep breath and let it out slowly, puffing his cheeks.

He had to shift mental gears, he thought. He was taking off his coaching hat and putting on his man-in-love hat. He was going to need his full concentration for the conversation he was about to have with Polly.

What he said and Polly's reaction to his words would determine his—their—entire future. Lord, what a daunting thought.

What if he blew it? He'd just executed the lousiest job of coaching of his entire career. What if he royally messed up his confrontation with Polly?

Knock if off, Dillon, he told himself. That was enough of the negative. He had to serve himself a dose of Pollyanna positive thinking.

Polly would listen, really hear, what he was saying to her. She'd agree to allow him to take over the financial obligation to her brother and sister. She'd accept his proposal of marriage and they'd live happily ever after. The end.

"Have you got that, Ms. Chapman?" he said.

Ah, Polly, he thought, *please.*

Polly sat curled up in the corner of the sofa, wearing a red flannel granny nightgown her mother had sewn for Polly's Christmas present the previous year.

She was watching *Sleepless in Seattle* on television, allowing herself to weep buckets during the touching scenes of the movie.

She was a masochist, she supposed, dabbing at her red nose with a tissue. The couple in the movie were going to have a happy ending in their relationship, just as they'd had the other five times she'd watched the film. They'd be together for all time, glowing with joy.

"And Polly Chapman?" she said. "Oh-h-h, I'm in the middle of a miserable ending to the glorious days and nights I had with Joe Dillon."

Polly reached for a fresh tissue, blew her nose, then tossed the soggy tissues into the wastebasket she'd toted into the living room from the bathroom.

When she'd gone into the bathroom to retrieve the basket, fresh tears had flowed at the sight of the curtain on the window that she'd used as a shawl on the night of her dinner date with Joe.

Everywhere she turned, it seemed, there was a memory of Joe waiting to haunt her.

A knock sounded at the door and Polly jerked in surprise.

"Oh, dear, dear," she said, glancing down at her granny nightgown attire.

Oh, who cared how she looked? she thought, slipping off the sofa. She was covered modestly from neck to toes, if she wanted to get technical about it. It was probably just one of her neighbors wishing to borrow something. Then again, it was rather late for a neighbor to come calling. But...

"Forget it," she said aloud, dashing the tears from her cheeks. "Just open the door, deal with whomever, and be done with it."

Dismissing her own rule of looking out the window to identify who was there, Polly flung open the door.

And then she stopped breathing as her eyes widened in shock.

"Hello, Polly," Joe said quietly.

Polly opened her mouth, then closed it and took a much needed breath.

"Joe?" she finally managed to squeak.

"May I come in?"

"Well, I... No, you can't. I'm...sick. I have a cold, the flu and...didn't Debbie and Jerome tell you that I was ill?"

"Debbie delivered a very lengthy message to me," he said dryly.

"Then why are you here? I have germs."

No, Joe thought, Polly had tears that were still shimmering in her expressive blue eyes. There she stood, the woman he loved, in her quaint nightgown, looking as if she'd just stepped off the page of a Victorian novel.

Her nose was red, her cheeks were blotchy from crying...she was beautiful, fantastic, exquisite. His.

"We have to talk," he said, stepping into the living room.

"But I'm contagious," Polly said, moving backward.

Joe closed the door and folded his arms over his chest. "Polly, you're not sick. You've been crying."

"Oh. Well, I always cry when I'm sick, because I hate being sick, and I feel very sorry for myself when I'm sick, so I cry."

"You're also a lousy liar."

Polly sighed. "That's what the police officer told me when I said I was Jerome's guardian."

"I rest my case. Shall we sit down?"

Polly threw up her hands in defeat and marched over

to the sofa, plunking down in the corner where she'd been indulging in her crying jag. She pressed a button on the remote control and shut off the television as Joe settled in the easy chair.

"Would you care to tell me why you're crying?" he said, looking directly at Polly.

"No."

"All right, then *I'll* tell *you*. You're crying, Polly Chapman, because you've come to realize that you're in love with me and you believe that it's impossible to pursue the hopes and dreams that emotion conjures up in your heart and mind."

"Don't be ridiculous," Polly said, poking her nose in the air. "I never said that I was in love with you, Joe Dillon. You certainly are full of yourself. You have an ego the size of the state of Texas."

"Is that a fact?" he said, propping one ankle on the opposite knee. "What about when you were at the house I intend to buy? What about the baby's nursery with the teddy bears and the music box? What about saying what a wonderful father I would be, then announcing how very much you loved me?"

"Oh…dear…heaven," Polly said, feeling a warm flush on her already blotchy cheeks.

Joe dropped his foot to the floor and leaned forward, resting his elbows on his knees and lacing his fingers.

"Yes, Polly, I heard everything you said in that room. Now I'm going to add my two cents' worth to that scenario." Joe paused. "Polly Chapman, I love you. I am deeply in love with you, and I'm asking you to marry me, be my partner in life, the mother of my children. Will you, Polly? Will you marry me? Please?"

Fresh tears spilled onto Polly's cheeks and she wrapped her hands around her elbows.

"I can't," she said, shaking her head. "Oh, why are you doing this to me? It will be so much more difficult to deal with knowing you actually love me. Joe, nothing has changed. I'm not free. I have…"

"Financial obligations for your brother and sister," he concluded for her. "I know that, and *you* know I'm willing to take care of the situation."

"No," she said. "No, I could never allow you to do that."

"Damn it, Polly," he said, lunging to his feet. "Would you quit selling yourself so short? It gets very tiresome after a while."

"What?" she said, obviously confused by Joe's outburst. "I'm what?"

"All your life," he said, frowning as he planted his hands on his hips, "you've had to settle for second best, and somewhere along the line you've come to the conclusion that *you* are second best, and you don't deserve to have it all—hopes and dreams, love and marriage—the whole nine yards."

"I…"

"Hear me out," he said, his volume rising. "I can't change your childhood, Polly, any more than I can make mine different from what it was. But we sure as hell can do something about our present and future. Why aren't you willing to do that, instead of just dwelling on how things were?"

Polly scrambled off the sofa. "How dare you?" she said, none too quietly. "You're dismissing my pride as though it were a worthless entity. I will not take your money to meet my obligations, Joe Dillon."

"You just don't get it," he said, dragging one hand through his hair.

"Me?" Polly said. "You're the one stubbornly refusing to face the facts."

"I'm facing the fact that you're hiding behind a protective wall, afraid to love, afraid to believe in hopes and dreams because of a lifetime of disappointments. And, I repeat, you're selling yourself short."

"That doesn't make sense. I'm selling myself short? That's nonsense."

"Is it?" he said, his voice suddenly very quiet and very low. "When two people pledge their love, make a commitment to forever—marry—they each bring what is uniquely theirs to that union. Do you agree with that statement?"

"Well," Polly said slowly, "yes."

"Good. The thing is, Polly, all you can envision about yourself is what you *don't* have to offer me. You get to the part about not being free because of your financial situation and you stop. Right there. Selling yourself short."

"But…"

"Let me finish. Don't you realize what you add to my life? You are sunshine itself, with your Pollyanna, look-at-the-bright-side attitude. You fill me up, make me happier than I've ever been in my entire life. You make *me* have hopes and dreams I never thought could be mine. You complete me, make me whole.

"And when we make love? Ah, Polly, it's so exquisitely beautiful I can't even find the words to describe it."

Polly pressed trembling fingertips to her lips to stifle a sob that threatened to escape.

"Polly Chapman," Joe continued, "you are my life. I want, I need, you to be my wife. But what am *I* bringing to our union? In my mind's eye it's only a fraction of what you give to me, but I hope, pray, it's enough.

"It's so damn incidental and unimportant that I have more money than you do. Yet you're allowing that fact to rob us of everything we could have together.

"I'm not belittling your pride. *You're* diminishing *yourself.* You're worth so much more than the few thousands of dollars it will take to help your brother and sister. God, Polly, can't you see that?"

Polly flattened her hands on her suddenly throbbing temples as Joe's words hammered in her head in a painful staccato.

"I...no, I..." She nearly choked on a sob. "You're confusing me. I can't think straight." Polly drew a shuddering breath as tears flowed unchecked down her cheeks. "You sounded so hurt and so bitter when you spoke of how your parents thought all problems could be solved with a checkbook. But now you're attempting to do the same thing."

"No, I'm not!"

Joe closed the distance between them and gripped Polly's shoulders.

"I'm not like my parents," he said. "This is a one-time thing that will make it possible for us to have a future together. We'll be living on my teacher's salary and whatever you make, for as long as you care to work. We'll be ordinary, middle-class citizens."

"And, oh, by the way, although it's hardly worth mentioning, you're helping put your wife's brother and sister through college?" Polly shook her head. "No. No, I can't do it. It's wrong."

"Damn it, Polly, don't do this to us," Joe said. "You're throwing us and everything we could have together away."

"I have no choice, Joe. I know who I am and what I have to do. I love you and I want it all, everything you spoke of, but it isn't mine to have. It just...it just isn't."

Through the mist of tears in her eyes Polly watched the shift of emotions cross Joe's face and settle in his dark eyes. She saw anger, frustration, weariness, then pain, raw pain, that seemed to come from the very depths of his soul.

"I guess there's nothing more I can say," he said, dropping his hands from Polly's shoulders and taking a step backward. "I fought the battle, and I lost. *We* lost." He stared up at the ceiling. "God, I don't believe this."

"I'm sorry, Joe," Polly said, crying openly.

Joe strode to the door, yanked it open, then half turned toward Polly.

"Goodbye, Polly," he said, his voice raspy with emotion. "Did I ever tell you that you remind me of a hummingbird? Did I tell you that? So delicate, yet so strong and...I love you, Polly. I just hope the day will come when I don't."

Joe left the apartment, closing the door behind him with a resounding slam that felt like a physical blow to Polly.

She reached out one hand blindly, groping for the sofa, then moving forward on trembling legs. She sank onto the faded, lumpy cushions and wept until no more tears would come.

And then she slept, dreaming of Joe.

The drive to his little house on the south side was a blur to Joe. He blanked his mind and drove by rote, not allowing himself to think or react until he was in his minuscule living room.

He sank onto the sofa, dragged both hands down his

face, then leaned his head back on the top of the worn fabric and stared at the ceiling.

It was over, he thought incredulously. He'd lost. He'd lost the only woman he'd ever loved. His hopes and dreams, all his plans for a future with Polly had been destroyed, blown away beyond his reach, into oblivion.

He would, he knew, replay that final scene in Polly's apartment over and over in his mind, wondering what he should have done, said, differently.

He'd searched his mind frantically for the proper words, the ones that would chip away at Polly's wall and bring her rushing into his arms, smiling through her tears, joyfully accepting his proposal of marriage.

"Yeah, right," he said, with a bitter sounding bark of laughter. "What a joke."

It was over.

It…was…over.

"Oh, Lord," he said, closing his eyes. "I lost my little hummingbird, my Pollyanna Polly, my love, my life, my wife."

Time lost meaning as Joe sat there, just sat there, the crushing weight of despair making it impossible to move.

On Monday morning, Polly arrived at the clinic earlier than usual, having been unable to stay one minute longer in the gloomy prison her apartment had become. To her surprise, Nancy and Robert were already there in the back room.

"Hello, Polly," Nancy said, smiling. "You must have been receiving mental signals from us. We called you to see if you could come in early, but you'd already left home, and here you are. We wanted to talk to you before we opened the clinic."

"Is something wrong?" Polly said, looking at Nancy, Robert, then back at Nancy.

"No, no," Robert said. "We discussed your conversation with Nancy and have a solution that we hope will make you happy and keep you with us."

"Conversation?" Polly said, frowning.

"Last Friday?" Nancy said, matching Polly's frown. "You expressed your discontentment at having to pamper the pets, read stories to them, and all that nonsense?" She paused. "Polly, are you all right? You're awfully pale, and you have dark circles beneath your eyes."

"Yes, I'm fine. I...I just haven't slept well for the past few nights. I apologize to you both for complaining about my duties here. Please, just forget that I said anything."

"Absolutely not," Robert said, "because you're right. You worked very hard for your degree and you're not being allowed to use your abilities the way you should. But as I said, we have a solution we hope will meet with your approval."

"Let's sit down," Nancy said.

The trio settled at the table. Jazzy's cage was sitting on the far end.

"Polly want a cracker?" the macaw squawked.

"No, thank you, Jazzy," Polly said absently, as she looked questioningly at Nancy and Robert.

"Give me the bird, Joe," Jazzy said, "and a bottle of beer."

"Cork it, Jazzy," Robert said, "or I'll cut off your supply of grapes."

"Wanna snuggle, bunny?" the bird said.

"Hush, Jazzy," Nancy said. "Polly, we were approached several months ago by a group of veterinarians who were opening a free clinic down on the south side.

They wanted us to volunteer some hours, but with our schedules being what they are, we just couldn't obligate ourselves to taking on more than we are doing.''

Polly nodded.

"We spoke with the head of the committee over the weekend," Nancy continued, "explaining that your degree enables you to do everything except perform surgery. Would they, we asked, be interested in having you at their clinic two days a week? Well, they would be thrilled to have you.

"We'd continue to pay your regular salary while you volunteer your time down there. We'd get a high school student in here to read *Goodnight Moon* and what have you to our spoiled guests. Well, sweetie, what do you think?"

Polly's hands flew to her cheeks. "Oh, my gosh, I'd be like a real veterinarian. I'd be really helping, really making a difference. Oh, this is wonderful, wonderful. Thank you so much. I don't know what to say. Oh, thank you.''

"I think she likes the idea." Robert smiled at Nancy.

"A bottle of beer!" Jazzy said.

"A bottle of champagne," Nancy said, laughing. "This calls for a celebration." In the next instant she sobered. "Polly, there's something we want to say to you, something we want you to know."

"Yes?" Polly said, her own smile fading.

"Robert and I can't begin to tell you how much we respect you for speaking up the way you did. We also apologize sincerely for not realizing we were wasting your talents.

"It took courage to do what you did by talking to me. We admire you so much for knowing your own worth and for refusing to sell yourself short any longer.''

Polly stiffened in her chair. "Selling myself short?" That was what Joe had accused her of doing. He'd said she was selling herself short in regard to what she would be bringing to his life, their relationship, their future together. "I'm not...selling myself short."

"Not at Dogwood Veterinary Clinic, you're not," Robert said. "If you carry over that attitude into all aspects of your life, it will be 'look out, world, Polly Chapman is going after what she wants and deserves to have.' Whew. I sure wouldn't want to be the one to stand in your way."

"Not in this lifetime," Nancy said, laughing. "Well, duty calls, folksies. Polly, I'm so delighted that we worked this all out."

"Yes, so am I," she said, her mind racing. "Thank you again, so very much."

Polly remained at the table as Nancy and Robert left the room.

"Oh, dear, dear," Polly said aloud, pressing her fingertips to her temples, "this is so confusing. I've got all this new data to sift and sort through. Oh, Joe, what have I done? Have I made a terrible mistake? Was I wrong?"

"Polly want a cracker?" Jazzy said.

Polly sighed. "No, Jazzy, not a cracker. I need answers. I suddenly have a multitude of questions, and I need answers."

During the next two weeks, Polly was happier than she'd ever been in her professional life. The busy hours at the free clinic, combined with her work at the Dogwood office, flew by, leaving her exhausted and fulfilled.

But when she arrived home each evening the loneliness, heartbreak and confusion dropped over her like a cold, dark shroud.

She missed Joe. She ached for Joe. She loved Joe Dillon, and cried more tears of misery as she sought the answers to the questions in her beleaguered mind.

On Friday of the third week of volunteering at the free clinic, Debbie and Jerome came into the converted store. Polly shrieked in delight and hugged them both until they yelped for mercy.

"How did you know I was here?" Polly asked the pair.

"News travels in this neighborhood," Jerome said. "Nothing much goes on that we don't eventually find out about."

"Coach Dillon is moving into his new house tomorrow," Debbie announced out of the blue.

"Oh," Polly said, feeling a painful knot tighten in her stomach. "Well, that's nice. Isn't that nice? Yes, indeed, that's very nice."

"So, why aren't you moving in there with him?" Debbie said.

Jerome rolled his eyes heavenward. "Here she goes again, messin' in people's business."

"Well, somebody had better," Debbie said. "Coach Dillon hasn't been fit to live with for weeks. The basketball team is still undefeated, but does Coach Dillon smile? No way. He just grumps around. Everybody knows he's got woman trouble. You're that woman, Polly, so fix things."

"It's not that simple," Polly said quietly.

"There's nothing complicated about loving somebody," Debbie said. "You either do, or you don't. If you do, you make it work between you. Right, Jerome?"

Jerome shrugged. "Makes sense to me."

"Hey, guess what, Polly?" Debbie rattled on. "Coach Dillon gave me and Jerome the furniture from his house down here. He's storing it for us at his parents' house until we get married. Can you believe that? We have our very own furniture.

"At first, you know, I said that we couldn't take it, like charity and all, but Coach Dillon set me straight on that in a New York minute."

"He did?" Polly said, hardly breathing.

"Sure enough," Debbie said, nodding. "He said it was just a small thing he was doing. He had something he didn't need, but we did. He said I shouldn't think it to death, just accept what he was offering. Don't sell yourself short, Debbie, he said, you deserve that furniture and much more. He's some kind of man, that Coach Dillon."

"Yes," Polly said, her eyes brimming with tears. "Yes, he is, and you are some kind of woman, Debbie. Thank you. Oh, thank you. I have my answers. Out of the mouths of babes. I adore you both."

"Huh?" Jerome said.

"What did I do?" Debbie said, obviously confused.

"You believe in yourself, and you listen when a wise man speaks," Polly said, smiling as she dashed two tears from her cheeks.

"Huh?" Jerome said.

The next afternoon, Polly drove slowly, very slowly, along the street where Joe's new house was located. She decreased her speed even more, hoping to muster more courage with each passing second.

She pulled into the driveway behind Joe's car and turned off the ignition of the van. As she stared at the house, a warmth suffused her as she envisioned the sunny rooms, the lovely fireplace banked by the bookshelves, and the precious nursery with the teddy bear motif and music box.

Joe's house, she thought. What happened within the next minutes within those walls would determine if the pretty brick structure would become Joe and Polly Dillon's home.

Taking a deep breath, she let it out to the count of ten. She checked her reflection in the rearview mirror, picked up her purse and a brown paper sack and opened the door to the van.

This was it, she thought, walking across the front lawn. Was she too late? Had she hurt Joe too much? Would he even listen to her, hear what she had to say? Was each step she took bringing her closer to shedding more tears from a shattered heart?

"Oh, dear, dear," Polly whispered, "this is terrifying."

On the porch, Polly saw that the front door had been propped open to no doubt make it easier for Joe to carry his belongings inside.

She peered into the living room from where she remained standing on the porch, smiling when she saw matching chairs in front of the fireplace. There were oak end tables in place with lamps centered on each.

Joe had marvelous taste in furniture, she thought. The living room was already appearing warm and welcoming, while only being halfway completed.

Joe, her mind echoed. Where was he?

"Hello?" she called. "Joe? Hello?"

There was no answering sound of Joe's voice.

"Go for it, Polly," she said, under her breath. "This is it."

She moved forward tentatively, acutely aware that she felt like an intruder who would not be made welcome.

Would Joe send her away without giving her a chance to speak from her heart? she thought, her step faltering. Would he point to the door and demand that she leave?

Get a grip, she admonished herself. Where was her Pollyanna outlook when she needed it? Where was the bright side hiding? The entire future rested on what was about to happen. She had to get herself together.

Polly squared her shoulders, lifted her chin and went on into the kitchen. No Joe. A sudden noise coming from the backyard caught her attention and she looked out of the open window over the sink.

"Oh, my," she said softly, "look at that."

Joe was laying flat on his back on the grass. Next to him, wiggling and yipping in excitement, was a golden retriever puppy that kept falling over its own feet, then bouncing up again to nuzzle and lick a chuckling Joe.

Polly drank in the sight before her, tucking it away carefully in her heart as a precious memory.

"Quit stalling, Polly," she whispered. "This is it. Oh, dear, dear."

She tightened her hold on the sack, hitched her purse strap higher on her shoulder and went to the back door. She opened it and stepped into the yard.

The puppy saw her before Joe did, the frisky animal bounding toward her, only to tumble and land upside down at Polly's feet.

"Hello, cutie-pie," Polly said, smiling down at the puppy.

Joe's head snapped around and he rolled to his feet in the next instant, absently brushing the dry grass from his behind.

"Polly?" he said.

This…is…it, Polly mentally repeated, then raised her head to meet Joe's gaze.

"Hello, Joe," she said, no hint of a smile on her face. "You picked out a marvelous dog."

"Yeah," he said, the wild tempo of his heart thundering in his ears. "He's fun. Not too coordinated at this point but... What are you doing here?"

"I...I'd like to talk to you, if you're willing to listen."

"All right," he said, frowning. "Go ahead. Talk."

"Could we go inside and sit down?"

Joe hesitated a moment, then nodded and started toward Polly.

Do not touch her, he ordered himself. *Do not haul her into your arms and kiss her. Do not dwell on the fact that you love Polly Chapman beyond reason. This woman hurt you, Dillon, sliced you into a million pieces. Remember that, damn it.*

The puppy was left in the yard and whined his disapproval. In the next moment he flopped down in a puddle of sunlight and went to sleep.

Joe edged around Polly and strode into the living room. She followed and he gestured to the chairs in front of the fireplace.

Polly sank onto one with an inward sigh of relief, knowing her trembling legs would not have supported her much longer. She placed the sack and her purse on the floor next to the chair.

"These chairs are lovely," she said, running one hand along the butter-soft leather arm.

"Mmm." Joe slouched onto the other chair and folded his arms across his chest.

So closed, so angry, Polly thought, looking over at him. And so very, very hurt, because of her.

She drew a steadying breath and clutched her hands in her lap.

"Joe," she said, wishing her voice was stronger, "I

know I hurt you deeply when I refused your proposal of marriage and sent you away.''

Joe lifted one shoulder in a shrug. There was no readable expression on his face.

''At the time I could see no other choice but to do what I did,'' Polly continued, ''even though…even though I love you so very much. But then I began to think, couldn't stop thinking, about what you said about selling myself short, about what I, as a person, a woman, could bring to our relationship.''

''Mmm,'' Joe said.

And? he mentally prompted, forcing himself to sit perfectly still. What was Polly leading up to? What had she really come here to say? *Easy, Dillon.* Polly had demolished him once. Maybe she'd shown up to get some kind of final closure for herself. *Don't hope. Don't dream, Dillon.*

''I stood up for myself at work,'' Polly said, bringing Joe from his racing thoughts. ''I told Nancy and Robert that I had more to offer than what I was being allowed to do there, and they fixed it. They agreed with me and set things to rights. I couldn't believe it.

''I'd buried my discontent at work for so long that I didn't even realize it was there until you helped me see it. I've grown, changed, now know I have the right to use the full potential of my abilities.

''Oh, Joe, I do have worth, I am important. I don't have to settle for second best for the rest of my life, simply because that's how it has always been.''

Joe shifted his hands to the arms of the chair and gripped the soft leather tightly, his gaze riveted on Polly.

''I was so confused, muddled,'' she continued. ''But just as it was Debbie and Jerome who made you realize you were wrong about your stand to live in the ghetto, they were the ones who gave me the answers I was so desperately seeking.''

Joe cleared his throat. ''Oh?''

''I've been hiding, Joe,'' Polly said, her eyes filling with unwelcomed tears, ''behind a protective wall that kept hopes and dreams at bay. Hiding like a frightened child who couldn't bear the thought of further disappointment.''

''I zeroed in on the issue of money, hung on to it like a lifeline, used it to keep us apart, because I was so terrified of dreaming, believing, we could have a wonderful future together.''

Polly lifted her chin, ignoring two tears that slid down her cheeks.

''Well, enough of that nonsense. I'm worth more than a few thousand dollars. I am capable of being a devoted wife, an equal partner, a wonderful mother. I have the fortitude to stand by your side until death parts us, in good times and bad, no matter what.

''I will never again sell myself short. I will never again stop believing in hopes and dreams. I love you, Joe Dillon, and if you can find it in your heart to forgive me for my foolishness, for the pain I caused you, then we can have it all.'' A sob caught in Polly's throat. ''Please, Joe?''

Joe moved so fast he nearly toppled over. He gripped Polly by the upper arms and pulled her from the chair to speak close to her lips.

''Do you mean it?'' he said, his voice raspy with emotion. ''Do you really mean it? Will you let me help your brother and sister through college, make money the unimportant issue it should be?''

''Yes, but...''

''But?'' he said, frowning.

Polly wiggled out of his grasp and reached into the sack. She pulled out a pink ceramic piggy bank, which she set on the hearth.

"I do have a smidgen of pride that is still in the way," she said. "I'll pay back every dollar you give to my brother and sister. It will go into the piggy, one penny at a time."

"Sold," Joe said. Whatever she wanted was fine with him. He was the luckiest and happiest man on the face of the earth. "Ah, Polly, I love you. I've missed you. This house is so empty without you and your sunshine. I need you here to make it a home. *Our* home. Will you marry me, Polly Chapman?"

"I certainly will, Joe Dillon," she said, smiling through her tears.

"Come here."

And Polly went.

She flung herself into Joe's arms and he captured her mouth in a searing kiss that ended the chill of loneliness and heartache and ignited the flames of passion.

Joe finally broke the kiss to draw a ragged breath.

"I brought one other thing with me," Polly said, her voice trembling with desire. "If you forgave me, if all our hopes and dreams were truly going to come true then…"

She moved out of Joe's embrace to take a fluffy teddy bear from the sack.

"It's a symbol of our future," she said, tears brimming her eyes again. "For the child we'll create with our love."

Joe reached out and took Polly's hand.

"I want to show you something," he said, urging her forward.

They went down the hallway to the room Polly had

envisioned as a baby's nursery. There on the floor in the empty room, sitting in a glowing circle of sunlight, was a music box with a smiling china teddy bear on top.

"Oh, Joe," Polly said, then sniffled.

"I don't know why I did it," he said. "You'd sent me away, it was over between us, but I couldn't let go, not entirely, of my hopes and dreams, of what might have been."

"Of what will be."

Polly walked into the room and sat the teddy bear next to the music box. She lifted the box, turned the knob, then set it back into place. The room was filled with the delicate music of a lullaby. She straightened and opened her arms to Joe.

And there in the room where the miracle, their baby, would sleep safe and warm, they made love.

They shed their clothes and reached eagerly for each other, sinking onto the plush carpeting, sunlight cascading over them. They kissed, caressed, rediscovered and gloried in all that they were, all they would give and receive.

Joe kissed Polly, parting her lips with gentle insistence, meeting her tongue, heightening their passion. Whispers of heat grew hotter, burning, as hands roamed, then lips followed the path taken.

Joe drew one of Polly's breasts deep into his mouth and her breath caught as wondrous sensations flowed throughout her. She splayed her hands on Joe's moist back, savoring the feel of his taut muscles, inhaling his aroma of fresh air and soap, her heart nearly bursting with love for this magnificent man.

I've come home, Joe, her mind whispered.

Welcome home, my love, Joe thought hazily.

They became one, united, meshed in body, hearts,

minds and souls. Committed to forever. Believing in hopes and dreams for all time.

The music box slowed, then stopped, but the litany singing in their hearts played on, accompanying them on their journey to ecstasy. They burst upon their glorious place seconds apart, calling to each other, holding fast.

Then they drifted down from the exquisite oblivion to a reality that was just as fantastic.

"I love you, Polly." Joe moved off her, but kept her close to his side.

"And I love you."

They sighed in contentment, hands resting on the other. Blissful minutes passed in sated silence.

"Joe?" Polly said finally.

"Hmm?"

"What did you name your dog?"

Joe chuckled. "There I was again, not wanting to forget you, the way we met."

"So what's the puppy's name?"

"Jazzy!"

Their mingled laughter danced through the air, filling the room to overflowing as it intertwined with their nearly tangible happiness.

Polly and Joe were so centered on the one they loved, they didn't see the magical moment when the fluffy teddy bear and the china one on the music box turned their heads to look at each other and nodded in approval.

*   *   *   *   *

DESIRE

AVAILABLE FROM 18TH FEBRUARY 2000

BLAYLOCK'S BRIDE Cait London

Man of the Month/The Blaylocks

A deathbed promise was about to bring Roman Blaylock face-to-face with the woman he longed for—the one woman he could never have. Could he persuade fiery Kallista Bellamy that he was a man she could trust?

HIS SECRET CHILD Beverly Barton

Many years ago, Sheila Vance became a woman in Caleb Bishop's arms. Now he's back in town and wants her back in his life—and bed. Only this time, Sheila's got a son to consider...

BELOVED SHEIKH Alexandra Sellers

Sons of the Desert

Just as Sheikh Rafi was about to steal his first kiss from bewitching Zara Blake, *she* was stolen from *him*, taken hostage by Rafi's archenemy! So now Rafi had to rescue the woman he wanted to make his queen...

LITTLE MISS INNOCENT? Lori Foster

Dr Daniel Sawyers was drawn to the one woman he disapproved of most, but Lace McGee had shown him nothing but steely resistance. Was the uncertainty in her gaze only to keep him at bay or was it to protect a secret innocence?

EXPECTING... Carol Grace

Mallory Phillips was pregnant, alone—and beautiful. Rugged Zach Calhoun was surprised by the strength of his desire as he watched her blossom. But could he see himself as a future father?

LET'S HAVE A BABY! Christy Lockhart

Jessica Stephens wanted a baby, so she asked Kurt Majors for a small, clinical *contribution*. Outraged, Kurt kidnapped her, resolving to teach her that babies should only be made the old-fashioned way...

0002/22a

AVAILABLE FROM 18TH FEBRUARY 2000

™ SILHOUETTE®

Sensation
A thrilling mix of passion, adventure and drama

ONE SUMMER'S KNIGHT Kathleen Creighton
WHEN YOU CALL MY NAME Sharon Sala
A HERO FOR ALL SEASONS Marie Ferrarella
NO SURRENDER Lindsay Longford
HERO UNDER COVER Suzanne Brockmann
FOR THE CHILDREN Margaret Watson

Intrigue
Danger, deception and desire

THE BRIDE'S PROTECTOR Gayle Wilson
THE MAN SHE MARRIED Dani Sinclair
RELUCTANT DAD Carla Cassidy
LONE STAR LAWMAN Joanna Wayne

Special Edition
Compelling romances packed with emotion

BABY, OUR BABY! Patricia Thayer
THE PERFECT NEIGHBOUR Nora Roberts
DADDY BY DESIGN Muriel Jensen
I TAKE THIS MAN—AGAIN! Carole Halston
THEIR MARRIAGE CONTRACT Val Daniels
A HERO AT HEART Ann Howard White

Look out in April 2000 for

A Fortune's Children Wedding

and the first book of a 5 part series

The Fortune's Children Brides

FREE!
2 Books
and a surprise gift!

We would like to take this opportunity to thank you for reading this Silhouette® book by offering you the chance to take TWO more specially selected titles from the Desire™ series absolutely FREE! We're also making this offer to introduce you to the benefits of the Reader Service™ —

★ FREE home delivery
★ FREE gifts and competitions
★ FREE monthly Newsletter
★ Books available before they're in the shops
★ Exclusive Reader Service discounts

Accepting these FREE books and gift places you under no obligation to buy; you may cancel at any time, even after receiving your free shipment. Simply complete your details below and return the entire page to the address below. *You don't even need a stamp!*

YES! Please send me 2 free Desire books and a surprise gift. I understand that unless you hear from me, I will receive 4 superb new titles every month for just £2.70 each, postage and packing free. I am under no obligation to purchase any books and may cancel my subscription at any time. The free books and gift will be mine to keep in any case.

DOEB

Ms/Mrs/Miss/Mr ....Initials ....

BLOCK CAPITALS PLEASE

Surname ....

Address ....

....

....Postcode ....

Send this whole page to:
UK: The Reader Service, FREEPOST CN81, Croydon, CR9 3WZ
EIRE: The Reader Service, PO Box 4546, Kilcock, County Kildare (stamp required)

Offer not valid to current Reader Service subscribers to this series. We reserve the right to refuse an application and applicants must be aged 18 years or over. Only one application per household. Terms and prices subject to change without notice. Offer expires 31st August 2000. As a result of this application, you may receive further offers from Harlequin Mills & Boon Limited and other carefully selected companies. If you would prefer not to share in this opportunity please write to The Data Manager at the address above.

Silhouette is a registered trademark used under license.

Desire is being used as a trademark.

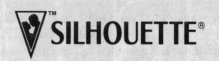

™ SILHOUETTE®

Maternity Leave

3 INDEPENDENT WOMEN
ARE EXPECTING BABIES...

...BUT HAVE MEN ON
THEIR MINDS!

CANDACE CAMP
TABLOID BABY

CAIT LONDON
THE NINE-MONTH KNIGHT

SHERRYL WOODS
THE PATERNITY TEST

Available from 18 February 2000

0003/30/SH1